THE BEST MAN'S SECRET

SPECIAL ILLUSTRATED EDITION

SPENCER BROTHERS
BOOK 3

ANA ASHLEY

Illustrated by

CARAVAGGIA

To all my readers that have been with me through novels and short stories, photo-filled newsletters and rambles.
Thank you for your support, dedication, and for helping me live my dream.
Yes, I am talking to you.
You're the best!

Ana

ABOUT THIS BOOK

Being the best man is hard. Being in love with the groom is worse.

A note under my door, and suddenly, I have to tell my best friend he's been jilted on his wedding day.
When it comes to Adam, there's nothing I won't do. I'll go on his honeymoon, invite him to live with me, and forget I'm keeping secrets that could destroy our friendship.

I've wanted Adam for years, and now it seems my feelings are less one-sided than I thought.
Crossing this line could cost everything. After all, there's a reason you shouldn't fall for your best friend—especially when he thinks he's straight.

The Best Man's Secret *is a steamy MM romance featuring childhood friends, forced proximity, bi-awakening, and a love brewing for decades.*
Expect romance, heat, fun, and secrets that won't stay hidden for long.

PROLOGUE
RIVER

Wedding Day

I WAS OFFICIALLY the worst best friend ever.

My hands shook as I held up the piece of paper that had been neatly folded and pushed under the door of my hotel room. A room that was far too big and luxurious for me, but Adam had wanted his best man close by, even if, so far, my main role had been to offer a place for him to hide from his groom obligations.

Why Victoria thought her introverted fiancé would enjoy multiple activities with people he'd never met—on his wedding weekend, no less—was beyond me.

I stared behind me at the closed door of my room, wishing I could hide inside instead of delivering the worst news a best man could to a groom. Adam's room was right across from mine. He was only a few feet away, oblivious to the fact his life was about to change.

When I saw the piece of paper, I panicked and went in

search of reinforcements. I'd bumped into Adam's identical twin brother Lex, his boyfriend Emery, and Emery's best friend Ellie. They'd seen the panic on my face before I spoke a word, so with the three of them on my heels, we'd gone to their older brother's room.

Noah had arrived from his honeymoon the night before, and while he was not the person I'd call on in a situation like this—because he was more likely to want to plot an assassination than provide any real help—his husband was. Older and definitely more balanced than all of us put together, Lior would be the voice of reason. He'd have the solution.

Right?

Except everyone had stared back at me when I told them about the note.

Someone had to tell Adam.

Apparently, that someone was me.

Okay, fine, this was what best friends were for, right? In kindergarten, when a kid took Adam's toy, I'd pushed the offender and told Adam we were friends now. I got grounded and wasn't allowed to play for the rest of the afternoon, but I also got a best friend.

Nine years after that day, my feelings for Adam would change. Not that he'd ever know it.

Don't worry, Adam. I will always have your back.

But did I? When I was also holding so many secrets?

What a stellar best friend I was.

1

———

ADAM

Three weeks ago

MY FINGERS HOVERED over the seating chart, a constellation of names and relationships spread before me. I shifted a place card, then moved it back.

I didn't dare touch anything on Victoria's side. She'd agonized for weeks about who would sit with whom at our wedding, who got to sit closer to our table or farther back. Now was my turn, except I didn't have a clue about the rules.

Apparently, where you sat at a wedding was important. You didn't want to cast Aunt Virginia to the Siberia of the seating chart because you'd forever hear about it at family gatherings, and god forbid you put the Wilson cousins at the same table. They were still not talking because of that one Christmas when they brought the exact same homemade pie for dessert and spent the evening accusing each other of buying it at a bakery.

This is ridiculous.

I pushed away from the table. With Victoria away for another business trip, I'd tried distracting myself with wedding stuff, but maybe what I needed was a break.

My wedding suit hung in the closet right next to River's. A classic midnight-blue tuxedo jacket with satin lapels, matching trousers with a pinstripe on the side, and a crisp white shirt.

River's was a copy of mine, which annoyed Victoria, who insisted the groom needed to stand out. I didn't want to stand out. I just wanted to marry her and grow old together, but that hadn't been the right answer.

She compromised by making River promise he'd only wear the jacket to the ceremony and would take it off for the photos and reception. I didn't tell her I didn't plan to wear the jacket all day either.

I ran my hands down the soft fabric. *Pick up the suits.* Another wedding task I'd completed today. Go me.

I smiled as an idea formed in my head. When was the last time we'd gone out just for shits and giggles?

A pre-bachelor party outing. That's what I needed. One last hurrah with my best friend before the whirlwind of the wedding swept us both away.

Before I talked myself out of it, because Victoria would be back tomorrow and hungover Adam was not her favorite, I grabbed my keys and headed for Lusitana.

The familiar route to my parents' restaurant calmed my nerves, even as a mix of emotions swirled in my belly. Something in the air was unsettling. If only I could pinpoint what it was. Probably just pre-wedding jitters.

Getting married? Hell yeah. Getting all the attention? Hard pass.

The dinner rush was in full swing when I arrived. I slipped through the crowded dining room. The controlled chaos of clattering pans and sizzling grills welcomed me, the scents of garlic and herbs filling the air.

The restaurant was as much home as our childhood home was, thanks to the endless school vacations my brothers and I spent working here. We'd mastered every single job except the kitchen. As teenagers, we'd felt like it was an obligation, but now I appreciated that Lusitana wasn't just a business. It was part of the family, and it was only when you got down and dirty with everyone else that you really understood why.

River had always loved it more than us, so my dad had taken him under his wing before we all left for college. He even got a business degree so he could one day take over the restaurant.

River was in his element at Lusitana. He moved with practiced grace, calling out orders and checking plates with a focused intensity that was River through and through.

"Hey, boss!" I called out, grinning as River's head snapped up in surprise. "Got a minute?"

His expression softened, a smile tugging at the corners of his mouth. "For you? Always," he said, wiping his hands on a towel as he approached. "What's up? Shouldn't you be cuddled up with your fiancée watching a movie or something?"

I shrugged, suddenly feeling a bit sheepish. "She's away for business."

River's brows furrowed. I knew exactly what he was thinking. Victoria had promised no business meetings during the month before the wedding.

Ignoring the words he wasn't saying, I said, "I had an idea. What do you say we blow this popsicle stand and have a guys' night out? Pre-bachelor party style?"

River's eyebrows shot up. "Now? Adam, I'm in the middle of dinner service. I can't just—"

"Come on," I pleaded, giving him my best puppy-dog

eyes. "When was the last time we did something spontaneous? I'm getting married in three weeks, man. Don't I deserve one last night of freedom?"

I watched the conflict play across his face and the moment responsibility gave way to something else. He sighed, shaking his head with a rueful smile. "You're impossible, you know that?"

"That's why you love me," I quipped.

River turned to his assistant manager, rattling off instructions and handing over the reins for the evening. I felt a surge of warmth at how easily he gave in. How willing he was to drop everything for me. It had always been that way between us, an effortless give and take that felt as natural as breathing. That was why he was my best friend.

As we stepped out into the cool evening air, I felt a weight lift from my shoulders. This was exactly what I needed—a night with my best friend, free from the pressures of wedding planning and future responsibilities.

"So, what's the plan?" River asked, falling into step beside me. "Please tell me it doesn't involve strippers or anything cliché like that."

I laughed, bumping his shoulder. "Give me some credit. I was thinking we could start with drinks at Tanner's and then maybe hit that new gay club that opened a couple of months ago."

River's eyes shot up at the mention of the gay club, but he didn't say anything. A club was a club, right? Music, alcohol, and poor decisions.

Besides, it's not like it would be the first time I'd been to a gay club. With my best friend and two brothers being queer, I'd been to more gay clubs than any other. I'd just never been the one suggesting it.

Cliffborough's city center was small enough that once you found your parking spot, you could walk everywhere, and thankfully for us, Tanner's wasn't far from Lusitana. The club was a little farther away, but we could get a rideshare back to get my car. If we got too drunk, we'd take the rideshare home and return for my car in the morning. Easy-peasy.

As we walked, I found my gaze drawn to River. The streetlights caught the angles of his face, softening the worry lines that had begun to appear. I frowned, wondering when those lines had formed and why I hadn't noticed them.

"You okay, River?" I asked. "You've got that look."

"What look?"

"The one that says you're overthinking something. Want to talk about it?"

"I want to talk about why you really came out tonight."

I didn't miss the shift in topic, but he was right. I *was* the one who'd sought him out. My hesitation was in how to articulate the mess of emotions coursing through me.

"I don't know," I admitted. "I'm excited about the wedding, I am. But there's this part of me that's… I don't know, sad? Like I'm losing something important."

River's steps faltered for a moment, his expression unreadable. "That's normal, I think," he said carefully. "Getting married is a big change. It's okay to feel conflicted about it."

"Yeah, maybe," I agreed. "Sorry, I didn't mean to get all heavy. This is supposed to be a fun night out, right?"

River's hand came to rest on my shoulder, warm and reassuring. "Hey, you know you can always talk to me about anything, fun night or not."

The sincerity in his voice made my throat tight. I covered River's hand with my own, giving it a grateful squeeze. "I know. Thanks, Riv. I don't know what I'd do without you."

Something flickered in his eyes, too quick for me to decipher. But before I could question it, River was smiling again, tugging me toward the welcoming glow of Tanner's. "Come on, let's get you a drink. I have a feeling you need it."

The bar was bustling with the Friday night crowd, but we managed to snag two stools at the far end of the bar. I ordered our usual and settled in, feeling the last of my tension melt away.

"So," River said, sipping his beer, "I hate to beat a dead horse, but how are the wedding plans coming along? Everything on track?"

I groaned, running a hand through my hair. "Don't even get me started. I never knew there were so many details to consider. Who knew that the color of napkins could be such a contentious issue? I spent hours today going through the seating chart. I'm not even sure I know half of those people."

River chuckled. "Let me guess, Victoria has strong opinions on table linens?"

"You have no idea."

"Well, if it isn't my favorite couple," Tanner said, appearing out of nowhere. I'd swear he hadn't been behind the bar when we sat down.

River rolled his eyes and asked, "What's up with you? Your husband working tonight, so you're out here pestering your best customers?"

"Nope. He's tied up to my desk in the office." He looked at his watch. "I'll give him an hour before I get back to finish what I started."

"Sorry I asked," River said at the same time I said. "Fuck that's hot."

River's head swung in my direction.

"What? Are you going to say it's not?" Edging wasn't something Victoria and I had done much of, but we were once interrupted by a work call during morning sex and ended up exchanging sexy texts all day. We didn't finish until later that night. Fucking best orgasm ever. I thought my head would blow off.

"Can we… Can we talk about something else? Please?"

I laughed. "Give us two more beers, Tanner. My friend here needs to cool down."

"Remind me again why was it such a good idea to abandon my job to hang out with you?" River asked.

"You love me and missed me."

"Sure I did." He drank the rest of his beer and put the empty bottle on the bar just as Tanner replaced it with a fresh one.

I leaned into River. "Let's drink up. We have a club to hit up. Let's show all the gays how it's done."

"Good lord. You really have no idea, do you?"

"About what?"

He quirked a brow as his lips curled up into a smile. "Without your brothers to run interference, you're going to be eaten alive in there, and I'm going to enjoy watching it."

2

―――

RIVER

As we stepped into the dimly lit club, the pulsating bass reverberated through my chest. Neon lights sliced through the darkness, and the air was thick with the scent of sweat and cologne, a heady mixture that made my head spin.

"This place is wild!" Adam shouted over the music, his blue eyes sparkling with excitement. "Come on, let's dance!"

I allowed myself to be pulled onto the crowded dance-floor, hyperaware of his warm hand clasped around my wrist. As we found a spot among the throng of dancers, my gaze was drawn to a couple nearby—two men moving in perfect sync, lost in each other's eyes. A familiar ache bloomed in my chest.

What would it be like to hold Adam that way? To run my fingers through that soft blond hair, to taste those full lips…

I shook my head, pushing away the useless thoughts. I'd lost count of the times I'd wondered if there was something more in the way Adam looked at me, only to get thrown back into the cold, harsh reality when he introduced me to yet another girlfriend over and over again.

"You okay?" Adam's concerned voice cut through my spiraling thoughts. "You seem distracted."

I forced a smile. "Just taking in the atmosphere," I lied because I couldn't confess he'd dragged me to my very worst nightmare.

As he moved to the pounding rhythm, my eyes roamed over his body. The way his hips swayed, how his T-shirt clung to his toned chest… It was intoxicating. And torturous.

My movements felt stiff and awkward in comparison. I'd never been much of a dancer, always too caught up in my own head. But Adam made it look so effortless, so natural. Like everything else in his charmed life.

A couple bumped into me from behind, jolting me out of my brooding. I stumbled forward, nearly colliding with Adam. Strong hands steadied me.

"Whoa there," he laughed, his breath warm against my ear. "Maybe the beers we had at Tanner's weren't enough. Let's grab another one, loosen you up a bit."

My skin tingled where he'd touched it. I swallowed hard, willing my racing heart to slow. "Yeah," I managed. "A drink sounds good."

As we made our way to the bar, my thoughts swirled with conflicting emotions. Desire and frustration. Longing and resignation. How much longer could I keep pretending I loved Adam only as a best friend? How much longer before these feelings tore me apart?

Hopefully not long now. Just three more weeks…

I wasn't naive enough to think those feelings would go away the moment Adam left for his honeymoon, ready to start his new life. A life that would include a wife. But I had a plan. All I could hope was that it would work.

As I leaned against the bar, catching my breath, a familiar voice cut through the din of the club.

"River? Is that you?"

I turned to see Mia, a regular at Lusitana, beaming at me. Her curly hair bounced as she pulled me into a quick hug.

"Mia! What are you doing here?" I asked, genuinely pleased to see a friendly face.

"Night out with my girlfriend." She winked. "But more importantly, what are you doing here? I thought clubs weren't your scene."

I chuckled, rubbing the back of my neck. "They're not, usually. I'm here with Adam." I gestured toward my best friend, who was chatting with the bartender.

Mia's eyes lit up with understanding. "Ah, I see. So, how's the restaurant doing? I'm craving your chocolate mousse something fierce. Work has been killing me lately. I miss my weekly fix of Lusitana's amazing Portuguese food."

"It's going well." I smiled. "We're actually planning a new seasonal menu. You should come by next week. I'll save you a portion of that chocolate mousse."

As we chatted, Adam returned with two drinks in hand. "Here you go, Riv. Oh, hey, Mia!"

"Adam! Long time no see." Mia grinned. "I was just telling River how much I miss the restaurant. Haven't seen your parents in forever."

Adam's face softened with pride. "You should come by. I'm sure Mom and Dad would love to see you."

"I'll do that. Besides, River has promised me some chocolate mousse. Well, I should get back to my girl," Mia said. "It was great seeing you both!"

As she disappeared into the crowd, Adam turned to me with a mischievous glint in his eye. "Ready to show off those moves, boss?"

I laughed, shaking my head. "You know I have two left feet, Adam."

"Drink up," he insisted, waiting patiently as we finished

the drinks before grabbing my hand and pulling me toward the dancefloor again. "I'll teach you."

"I'm not drunk enough for this," I groaned. "Can I get another beer?"

"Nope."

As we found a spot among the sea of bodies, Adam placed his hands on my hips, guiding me to the rhythm. My breath caught in my throat at the closeness.

"Just feel the beat," he said, his blue eyes twinkling. "Let go."

Slowly, I began to relax, letting him lead me. Our bodies moved in sync, years of friendship translating into an easy, natural flow.

"See? You've got it." He grinned, spinning me around playfully.

I laughed, genuinely enjoying myself for the first time in a while. "I so don't got it, but I see it's not too bad once you get into it," I replied.

As we danced, I allowed myself to revel in the moment. For now, I could just be here with my best friend, moving to the music and pretending this was enough. That I wasn't on the cusp of making a life-changing decision that could alter everything between me and Adam.

The pulsing lights of the club shifted, casting a warm glow across his face. My breath caught as our eyes locked, the world around us fading. A surge of desire coursed through me, electric and overwhelming. Adam's hands were still on my hips, our bodies swaying together, and I felt as if I might combust from the intensity of my longing.

"You okay?" Adam asked, his words barely audible over the music.

I nodded, not trusting my voice. I was acutely aware of every point of contact between us, of his scent mingling with the heavy air of the club.

"I'm going to get another drink. You want one?" I asked.

"Fuck yeah."

For the next few hours, we drank, danced, and lost track of time like we had in college. We were definitely way beyond buzzed. Thank fuck we'd walked because there was no way we were in any state to drive anywhere.

Suddenly, a strikingly tall man with a sharp jawline and long hair cascading down his broad shoulders appeared beside us, his piercing hazel eyes fixed on Adam. "Hey there, handsome," he purred, placing a hand on Adam's arm. "Care to dance?"

I felt my stomach drop, a familiar ache settling in my chest. That was my first instinct because I was always left behind. But even in my alcohol daze, I realized this was a guy hitting on Adam and he might not like that.

"Thanks, but I'm good here," Adam said, flashing the man a polite smile before returning his attention to me.

The guy's expression soured. "Come on, surely you'd rather dance with me than your friend?"

I tensed, preparing for the guy's reaction. But Adam just shook his head, his blue eyes never leaving my face.

"Sorry, but I'm exactly where I want to be," he said firmly.

As the guy huffed and walked away, a mix of relief and confusion washed over me. "You handled that really well," I said softly.

Adam's brow furrowed. "Handled what?"

"Turning him down. A guy like that is probably not used to being rejected."

His expression softened. "Meh. He was a six at best. Besides, I'm here with you. That's all that matters. I'm not leaving my best friend behind to dance with some random dude."

His reply shocked me into silence. Or maybe the alcohol

had the opposite effect on me than Adam because his lips seemed to be way looser than usual.

The music's pulsing beat faded as we made our way to a secluded corner of the club. I hadn't changed out of my work clothes, so my shirt, even with the sleeves rolled up, had way too much fabric for a club.

We sank into a plush leather booth, the cool material giving temporary relief.

Adam slid in next to me, our thighs barely touching. "This was a great idea. Thank you for letting me drag you away from work."

I would do anything for you. I smiled because I couldn't say what I really wanted to.

"You know," he said softly, his eyes half-lidded as he almost slurred the words, "I've always admired how deeply you care about people. You're so…intentional about everything."

My breath caught in my throat. "Yeah?"

He nodded, a small smile playing on his lips. "Absolutely. You put so much thought into every relationship, every inter-action. Even clients from the restaurant treat you like a friend. It's…beautiful, really."

The word beautiful hung in the air between us. That was the word I would use to describe everything about my best friend, from the way he looked to how he loved his family to the way he crafted words for the PR campaigns he worked on with his brothers. My fingers twitched, aching to reach out and touch his face, trace the curve of his jaw.

"I just wish…" I started, then hesitated. I couldn't…

"What is it?" He leaned closer, his knee brushing against mine under the table.

My heart pounded so loudly I was sure he could hear it. I opened my mouth, the words *Don't marry Victoria because I love you, and I know I can make you happier* balanced on the tip of my tongue. But fear gripped me, squeezing my chest.

"I just wish it was easier sometimes," I said instead. "To connect with people, you know?"

Adam's expression softened with sympathy. "I can only imagine. But hey, you've got me, right? Always."

I forced a smile, even as my heart twisted. "Yeah, I've got you."

3

———

RIVER

Wedding Day

THE DOOR OPENED, and I jumped.

"What are you doing out here, mumbling to yourself? I'm the one who's meant to be nervous. Fuck. I'm getting married today. Can you believe that?"

I stared at Adam. His navy suit fit him perfectly, but his hair was styled too neatly. His socks didn't match. One was white and the other gray. Had he noticed?

"River?" he called again.

"Yes. Sorry…may I come in?"

He pulled my hand and dragged me in, closing the door behind us.

"Why aren't you dressed yet?" He walked over to the floor-to-ceiling mirror in his room and started playing with his tie, redoing what had already been a perfect knot.

"Adam, I…" Fuck, I couldn't do this. Victoria's cowardly

letter burned in my hands, reminding me of my job. I had to break Adam's heart in her place.

My heart, I didn't care much about. It was permanently damaged. I'd accepted that a long time ago. But Adam's? His was precious.

I had to remember I was just the messenger. This wasn't my fault.

"What's up?" he asked, turning to face me.

A knock on the door made us both startle.

"Adam, honey? Can I see you?" his mom called from the other side of the door.

He took the few strides to the door, and as soon as he opened it, his mom ran into his arms.

"Oh, my baby. You look so handsome."

"Thanks, Mom. Everything okay?" he asked.

"Of course. I just wanted to see you before everything got a little crazy. Your dad and grandma wanted to come over, but I didn't want to put all the pressure on you. If you're anything like your dad, you'll be nervous enough. On our wedding day, he…" She started but shook her head before finishing her thought. "Those are memories for another day. Today is all about you and Victoria."

She straightened his already-straight tie. Her loving gaze as she cradled her son's cheeks spoke of nothing but pure love and pride.

Carla was an amazing woman and an even better mom. I should know. After all, I'd practically lived in the Spencer household since I was five, and now, as the manager of the restaurant, I spent enough time with her and Adam's dad.

Not that life at home had been bad, but with my mom working all the hours as a nurse at the hospital, I'd sometimes felt like Adam's family was my real family growing up.

She turned to me. "River Charles Hartley, what are you

doing *not* in a suit? And I don't want to hear any excuses about work. We closed the restaurant so you can enjoy the wedding and not worry. Do I need to have a word with Jack?"

I smiled. "It doesn't take me long to get ready, Carla. I promise I won't do any work today."

She was right to worry. I'd been using work as a crutch for the last eighteen months, and my plan to stop involved… nothing I could afford to think about right now.

"Well, I'll leave you boys to get ready," she said. "Adam, honey, do you want me to send something up for you to eat?"

"Thanks, Mom. I had room service earlier."

"Okay, in that case…" She gave us each a kiss on the cheek and left.

The click of the door closing shut sounded like a shotgun to my stomach.

You've got this.

Adam dropped on the couch in the suite. "Fuck, I need a coffee. Probably not the best thing to have when I'm already so nervous."

I sat next to him, trying to find the guts I didn't have.

"What's that?" he asked, pointing at the paper in my hand. "No, don't tell me. You wrote my vows because no one could trust me, *someone who crafts words for a living*, to do it myself."

"Probably because up until two days ago, you were still rewriting them," I said. "Not that you'll need them now."

"What do you mean?"

I held the paper up to him. He took it, his eyes filled with curiosity.

I couldn't look at him while he read the letter, but I heard the intake of breath with every word. The gasp. The questions. Until it was just silence.

Dear Adam

I know you're going to hate me for this, and you have every right to feel that way. Please know that I love you, and because of that, I have to do this.

I can't marry you today.

Out of all the awful things I've done in my life, this is by far the worst. I know that.

I'm so sorry I'm leaving you to deal with the fallout. You don't deserve it, but I'm selfish, and I know I can't be there and handle the disappointment.

You have everyone around you. They'll help.

I won't ask for your forgiveness, but I hope you can someday understand why I've made this choice.

Love,

Victoria.

Slowly and reluctantly, I raised my eyes. Adam's hands shook as he gripped the paper until his fingers were white.

"I'm sorry," I said, barely a whisper, wanting to reach out and put my arms around him.

I'd never seen my best friend look so…lost, destroyed, betrayed.

"Sh-she's gone," Adam stammered, the sentence a blade that cut through the last thread of hope. The paper crinkled in his tightening grip.

"Hey, hey, look at me," I urged gently, reaching out to steady his shaking shoulders. "We'll get through this. I'm here for you, okay?"

"How did you get this?" he asked.

"It was under my door this morning. My guess is it was put there before I woke up."

"Does anyone else know about it?"

I cringed. "Your brothers, Emery, Lior, and Ellie. I'm sorry. I didn't know what to do."

He stood and paced the room.

"I need to…" He ran his hands through his tidy hair, messing it up and making it look a lot more like my Adam. I wanted to smile at that but stopped myself. This wasn't the time to put my feelings first. My feelings didn't come into this equation at all.

I stood and reached out to him. Placing my hands on his shoulders, I said, "What do you need from me, Adam? What can I do?"

"Take me home. I need to… She might be at the apartment." With every word, his resolve hardened. I got it. He needed answers. He couldn't stay in limbo, halfway between married and single, without understanding why.

"Are you sure?"

He glanced at the digital clock on the side table and met my gaze with determination. "We have time. I need to try, River. I can't just let this happen like this. I don't know if she doesn't want to get married today…or at all. Why this? Why now? I can't—"

I placed my hands on his cheeks, making him face me so there was no doubt about my role in all of this. "We'll do whatever you need, okay?"

He nodded, his eyes turning red and moist.

"I'm not crying, okay?"

"I know, buddy. It's allergies. Let's get you home."

4

ADAM

My hands trembled as I looked for the car keys before remembering Victoria had kept them when she moved to the bridal suite. I looked out the window toward the parking lot. The sleek rental car that had sat pretentiously in the lot yesterday was now gone.

Victoria had taken that too.

"Come on, I'll drive," River said.

As I slid into the passenger seat, my pulse thrummed in my ears. I took a moment to lean against the seat, allowing myself one deep, shuddering breath.

I kept my head down as River drove us out of the vineyard.

Victoria had picked this place, the date, the flowers, the food, everything. I had been involved in the wedding planning, but Victoria had been very particular about what she wanted.

I'd taken all the ribbing from my family about *not helping* Victoria when, in fact, there was very little I could do right in her eyes.

And now…

"Are you sure you want to do this?" River asked for the hundredth time.

I let out a breath. "What would you do in my place?"

"I don't know."

He kept his eyes on the road, but his presence alone was enough to ground me.

It sucked that my brothers and their partners had found out about the collapse of my almost marriage before I did, but I don't think I could have heard it from anyone except River. I also couldn't blame River for going to my brothers for help. Victoria put him in an impossible position.

He was my best friend, the guy who had my back. Always. He knew how to read me as if he'd written the words of my book himself.

People made fun of us all the time, saying he was mine and Lex's triplet, but he wasn't. Lex and I were twins. We had a bond I could never describe to anyone in a way they'd understand. What River and I had was a deep friendship. The kind that would survive anything and last forever. It was almost the same but different.

The drive back to Cliffborough was a blur—the winding roads, once a picturesque journey, now felt like an endless loop of confusion and speculation. What had gone wrong? Had there been signs I missed, words unspoken, feelings ignored? I riffled through my memories, trying to find a trigger, anything that might give me an answer.

Fuck, less than twenty-four hours ago, she'd given no indication that anything but our perfect wedding would be happening. Or had I missed it?

We'd barely seen each other between the multiple events Victoria had organized this weekend. By the time she returned to the room each night, I was already asleep. The excuse in the morning was that she'd been up late with her bridesmaids.

Before she moved to the bridal suite, she'd kissed me. Had there been any clues in the kiss? Was it longer or shorter than usual? I couldn't remember.

Arriving at our place, the familiarity of the setting offered no answers. The apartment where we'd planned our future together, where we laughed and sometimes cried, now felt hollow in the wake of her absence.

"Victoria?" My voice sounded foreign in the quiet hallway as I opened the front door, the sound of my call bouncing off the walls, unanswered. I scanned the space frantically, searching each room meticulously with rising desperation. Her belongings seemed untouched, the silence of the apartment amplifying my racing thoughts.

When I stepped into the living room, I was faced with my honeymoon suitcases. Where four suitcases had been left, now there were only two. And a note.

Adam, this is on me. Please don't feel pressured to move out.

I'm going away for a while to reset.

We can talk when I return. Maybe then I'll have the courage to explain what I've done.

My knees gave out, and I fell to the floor, the piece of paper crumbling in my hands.

"Adam, what's wrong?" River asked, kneeling on the floor beside me.

"It's happening. It's true."

"What is?"

"She's really gone." My voice failed as a sob wrenched out of me. Tears streamed down my cheeks, blurring my vision as I looked at the crumpled note in my trembling hands.

River's arms came around me, his steady grip anchoring

me. We stayed in that position until my feet became numb from sitting on them.

I shifted so I was against the wall with my knees drawn up to my chest. I moved my feet to get rid of the pins and needles. River sat beside me.

"I don't know what to do next, River. Maybe it's the final piece of evidence that proves how desperate and gullible I am. I really thought she'd be here. That I'd get some answers or closure. I don't know."

"You are none of those things, Adam. You are an amazing guy. Anyone would be lucky to be with you."

"It seems Victoria doesn't feel the same way."

River's silence was louder than any words he could have said. There'd always been an unspoken tension between Victoria and River. I suspected it came from both, but Victoria was more outspoken about it, going as far as telling me I should stop hanging out with my best friend because he was a bad influence.

That should have been a red flag right there. Further proof that I was even more oblivious than gullible.

"I don't know what to say right now, Adam. Nothing I'm thinking is honestly a nice thing. I don't want to add to your stress and grief, so I'm just going to ask what I can do for you. What do you need right now?"

"I need to get out of here."

River stood and held his hand out to me, pulling me to my feet. He grabbed the suitcases and dragged them to his car.

I kept my eyes down as I left the apartment, locking the door behind me because I couldn't face looking at the place that had been home for the last year as Victoria and I built our dream life. What I'd thought was our dream life. Only to now see nothing but deception. I would have to return for my stuff, but it didn't need to be on my wedding day.

"Where do you want to go?" River asked.

"The last place I want to be. Take us back to the vineyard."

He put a reassuring hand on my leg. "Adam, your family can take care of everything. Your brothers will do anything for—"

"I know, but I'm not Victoria. I'm not going to run."

"Okay." That's all he said before pulling out of the driveway and heading back toward the venue. I pulled out my phone and messaged Lex.

ME

I need your help.

LEX

Is this a CODE RED situation?

ME

No. She doesn't get to ruin CODE RED for me. Can you tell Mom, Dad, and Grandma?

LEX

I can. Where are you? We've been to your room and you're not there. It's been hard trying to keep Mom calm. She thinks you got cold feet.

Now *that* was funny.

ME

No cold feet, just the rug pulled from under them.

LEX

Oh, Adam. I'm really sorry about this.

ME

Yeah. Can't say I had this on my Bingo card for today. Can you and Noah gather all the guests in the reception hall? I'm on my way there.

LEX

Leave it with us.

Seeing everyone inside the large room beautifully decorated for the reception was a hit to the gut. This was really happening. Or *not* happening, as was the case.

As soon as my mom saw me, she came straight over. Confusion and worry were etched all over her face.

"Adam, honey. What's going on?"

"I wish I knew, Mom. I have to make the announcement, okay?"

She hugged me tight and then went back to where the rest of my family sat together. The looks my brothers were sending Victoria's side of the family made me smile a little. Victoria's sister Ellie sent me a reassuring look.

Ellie was Emery's best friend, and I knew she and Victoria didn't have the best relationship. Just another flag I'd ignored.

"I'm not sure about this," River said in a low voice. "Noah looks like he might be ready to murder someone."

"Lior will keep him on a leash. Don't worry." I grabbed a chair and stood on it, clearing my throat.

Hundreds of faces turned in my direction. There were smiles, followed by confusion, when it dawned on them that this wasn't the good type of announcement.

"Hello, everyone. You might be wondering why you were asked to come to this room instead of heading outside to the garden where the ceremony should take place. I'm not going to sugarcoat it. The truth is that this morning, Victoria decided she no longer wanted to go ahead with the wedding."

The collective gasp gave me a weird sense of comfort. Since Victoria hadn't included me in her decision, there was no way I was going to take the fall for it. This was her decision and her decision alone.

I raised my hand before people started asking questions.

"I understand you may have questions. Frankly, I was in my room getting ready to marry the woman I love when I found out from a piece of paper that she no longer wants the same. I haven't spoken to her because I haven't seen her. No words can accurately describe how I feel right now. I hope you can find it in you to not give in to the curiosity you may feel or to feed the gossip mill, which I'm sure is already running wild. Whatever Victoria's reasons for doing this, they are her reasons, and it'll be up to her to tell her story when and if she wants to. As far as I'm concerned, our relationship is over because that's what this"—I held up the two pieces of paper with Victoria's messages—"tells me. Everything else is as much a mystery to you as it is to me.

"Right now, I want to be alone to process what has happened today. I apologize from the bottom of my heart for what has happened. While the wedding is no longer going ahead, there's no point in wasting a perfectly good party. Please feel free to enjoy the catering and the facilities. The team at the vineyard has been amazing, and I'm sure they will continue to do their best to accommodate you. Please forgive me for not joining you."

5

———

RIVER

I trailed behind Adam, my eyes fixed on his rigid shoulders. The usual carefree warmth in his demeanor had vanished, replaced by an unsettling detachment that sent a chill down my spine.

"Adam, wait up," I called softly, quickening my pace to catch up. "Are you okay?"

Adam paused at his room door, key card hovering over the lock. He turned around, his eyes uncharacteristically distant. "I'm fine," he replied, his voice flat. "Just need a minute."

I hesitated as he swung the door open, torn between giving him space and my instinct to comfort him. Before I could decide, Adam gestured for me to enter.

"Please don't leave me alone to face the firing squad. Even if their intent is to fire on my behalf and not at me."

How could Adam be so calm after what just happened? This wasn't like him at all. I watched as he methodically removed his suit jacket and loosened his tie, movements precise and controlled.

"Adam, you don't have to pretend with me," I said gently, leaning against the wall. "It's okay to be upset."

His gaze met mine, a flicker of emotion finally breaking through. "I don't know what I am right now, Riv. It's like I'm on the outside, watching everything happen to someone else."

My heart ached at the vulnerability in Adam's voice. So many times in my life, I'd wished I could just kiss him and take care of him. Make all the hurt go away. But if that little wish had come true, there's no way he'd be hurting this way. Not on his wedding day. Not ever.

I stepped forward, hand outstretched, when a knock at the door interrupted the moment.

"Adam? Honey, it's Mom and Dad. Can we come in?"

As Adam had predicted, his parents entered, followed closely by Lex, Emery, Noah, and Lior. The room suddenly felt crowded, filled with concerned faces and hushed voices.

"Oh, honey," Adam's mother said, rushing to embrace her son. "We're so sorry this happened. Are you all right?"

He returned the hug mechanically, his eyes meeting mine over his mother's shoulder. "I'm okay, Mom. Really."

Lex stepped forward, placing a hand on Adam's arm. "We're all here for you, bro. Whatever you need."

"Thanks," he replied, his voice soft. "I appreciate it, all of you."

As the family crowded around Adam, offering words of comfort and support, I found myself retreating to the corner of the room, watching the scene unfold, feeling both a part of and separate from the family unit.

Whenever his gaze drifted to me, I offered small, reassuring smiles, even as my own emotions churned beneath the surface.

I should have been happier that the wedding was off, but

my immediate guilt for the selfish thought made me feel like the worst friend in the world. Today already felt a week long, this morning only a distant memory. One that wouldn't be erased from my brain anytime soon.

Noah's voice cut through the conversation, sharp and angry. "We should make her pay for this. I know a guy who—"

"Noah!" Adam's father interjected, his tone firm. "That's not the answer. We'll handle this the right way."

"I'm not one to enable Noah's weird ideas, but Victoria was really mean to Emery when we reconnected, so…" Lex said, putting his arm around Emery's waist.

Emery shook his head. "It was a while ago, and it doesn't matter."

"Baby, she's hurt two of the people I love the most in the world. She can't get away with it."

"Hear me out," Noah said.

"Here we go," Lior interjected. "I apologize in advance, and if you want me to tie him up somewhere for a while so he can't get into trouble, I'm sure it could be arranged."

"Ooh, kinky, but, babe, not in front of my family. They already know far too much about our sex life."

Lior closed his eyes and took a deep breath. Seeing them together made so much sense. The older, more controlled man was perfect to balance out Noah's wild side.

"As I was saying," Noah continued, "I know a guy who, for a small fee, will do a bunch of stuff. Nothing illegal. You still have your apartment key, right, Adam?"

Adam nodded.

"So the guy goes in and replaces all the shampoo in the bottles for soap with glitter. He hides all the left shoes, apart from any smelly, dirty sneakers. He replaces the cutlery with spoons and can check your TV and delete all the shows you have saved. If you want to be reeeally petty, you can sign Victoria up for all kinds of magazine and email subscriptions and list her phone number on Craig's List as an advice columnist for weird body problems."

"Hmm, I've got to admit those are not bad ideas," Emery said.

I watched as Adam remained quiet, almost detached, a storm brewing behind his blue eyes.

"Just say the word, little brother, and I'll get on it," Noah said.

Lior pulled Noah close. "I worry about you sometimes."

"It's okay, baby. I know you'd never do anything to trigger my enthusiasm for the road less traveled."

"Noah, I went away on a work trip and came home to a dog."

Noah grinned. "Yeah, but that was cute Noah."

"There's nothing to handle," Adam said suddenly, his voice surprisingly steady. "The wedding's off. Victoria made her choice, although it would have been much less embarrassing if she'd done it before this morning. No point in agonizing over it. I need a break from this so I'm going to go on my honeymoon, since I paid for it and all. When I'm back, I'll deal with the rest."

A hush fell over the room. My breath caught, surprised by Adam's declaration.

His mother stepped forward, brow furrowed with worry. "Sweetheart, are you sure that's a good idea? After everything that's happened…"

Adam's gaze met mine, and for a moment, I saw a flicker of the determination I knew so well. "I'm sure, Mom. I won't let Victoria take this from me too."

I found myself nodding, a surge of pride and affection washing over me. This was the Adam I knew—resilient, stubborn, refusing to be beaten down.

"But you shouldn't go alone," Lex chimed in, concern etched on his face.

Adam's lips quirked in a small smile, the first I'd seen since the wedding disaster. "Who says I have to?"

His eyes locked with mine again, and I felt a jolt of electricity run through me. What was he thinking? And why did that look make my belly tighten?

Adam's smile widened, a mischievous glint appearing in his eyes. "You know what? River, Lex, Emery, Noah, Lior, you should all come with me."

I blinked, caught off guard by his sudden shift in mood. The others seemed equally surprised, exchanging confused glances.

"Are you serious?" Noah asked, his eyebrows raised.

Adam shrugged, his demeanor unexpectedly light. "Why not? It's already paid for. Might as well make it a family vacation, right?"

I couldn't help but marvel over his resilience. Here he was, hours after being jilted, suggesting we all crash his honeymoon. It was so absurd, so utterly Adam, that I felt a burst of warmth in my chest.

"Hell yeah!" Noah exclaimed, a grin spreading across his face before he turned to his husband. "We're in. What do you say, Mr. Van Spencer? Fancy another honeymoon?"

Lior laughed. "With you? Any time. Let me make a couple of phone calls." Giving his husband a kiss on his temple, Lior pulled out his phone and walked to the balcony.

As the others began to chatter excitedly, I caught Adam's eye. He watched me, his expression a mix of hope and something I couldn't quite place. My heart stuttered, and I found myself wondering what it would be like to spend a week with him in paradise.

"What do you think, River?" he asked softly, his voice barely audible over the commotion. "You in?"

I swallowed hard, torn between the longing to be there for my best friend and the nagging fear that this would make me change my mind about the plans I'd been working on for the last few months. But as I looked at Adam, his eyes pleading, I knew there was only one answer I could give.

I took a deep breath, steadying myself. "Of course I'm in," I said, "Someone's got to make sure you don't drown your sorrows in too many Mai Tais."

His face lit up with a grin, and I felt my heart skip a beat. "You're the best, River," he said, squeezing my shoulder. The warmth of his hand lingered even after he pulled away.

As the others continued to make plans, I found myself lost in thought. What was I getting myself into? A week in paradise with Adam, surrounded by couples on their honeymoons…? It felt like a recipe for heartache. But I couldn't bring myself to regret my decision, not when my best friend needed me.

An hour passed in a blur of phone calls and excited chatter. Lior finally hung up his phone and turned to address the group. "All right, everything's set," he announced. "We've got a private jet leaving tomorrow morning, and since Adam already has the honeymoon suite, I've booked two additional suites."

I nodded, relieved that things were falling into place. But then Lior continued, "The only hiccup is that there aren't any extra rooms available. River, our suite has a pull-out couch, and it's big enough that we won't be on top of each other. You're more than welcome to stay there."

My stomach dropped. The thought of being so close to Adam yet still separated felt like a cruel joke. But before I could respond, Adam spoke up.

"No way," he said firmly. "River's not sleeping on some uncomfortable couch. He can stay with me in my suite. We shared a room in college. It'll be just like old times."

I froze, my mind reeling. Just like old times?

If only Adam knew how different our experience of sharing the same room had been for me. But as I met his earnest gaze, I found myself nodding. "Yeah," I managed to say, my voice slightly hoarse. "Just like old times."

6

———

ADAM

A sliver of sunlight pierced the semi-darkness of the room. For a moment, I lay still, listening to the world outside. The distant chirping of birds and the occasional duck quack.

I pressed a hand against my chest, feeling a dull throb, the memory of yesterday's events playing over and over in my head—the pain, the pity in my family's gazes as I announced the wedding cancellation to our guests.

Time to move on.

I swung my legs off the bed, my feet meeting the cool floor. I stood, stretched my arms above my head, and took a deep, resolving breath.

Today would not be about what-ifs or might-have-beens. Today was for moving forward, for reclaiming the narrative of my own life. I was going to Maui for a honeymoon, and dammit, I was going to have one—Victoria or no Victoria.

My phone vibrated against the nightstand, the screen lighting up with a message from River.

RIVER

Skipping the vineyard breakfast. Meet in the lobby?

I exhaled a silent thank you, grateful for the excuse to avoid the sympathetic stares and hushed whispers.

ME

Sounds good.

By the time I arrived at the lobby, River was already there, leaning casually against the wall, his green eyes scanning the room until they landed on me. Maybe I was already giving out my ready-for-change aura because the corners of his mouth lifted in a small smile.

"Where are the others?" I asked.

"Noah and Lior are outside. Lex and Emery are on their way down."

"Great. I'll just go check out."

"No need. Drop your room keys in that box by the reception desk. Your parents took care of the rest. I caught them on the way to breakfast. They said to have a great time and don't let Noah murder anyone for the love of god. They also said marry, but I think Lior has that part covered."

I laughed. "No murders. No marriages. Fun. Got it."

My life wasn't exactly going according to plan, but I had the best family in the world. When Victoria said in her note that I'd have everyone around me, she'd been right.

As we walked outside to each of our cars—my brothers in theirs and me with River—all I felt for Victoria was pity. She could have had all this, but instead, she chose to walk away.

Maybe one day I'd have answers, but right now, with my family around me, I was okay. More than okay. I was on my way to freakin' Hawaii for an all-expenses-paid vacation.

Thank you, Past Adam!

Another Past Adam great decision was to get my brothers to come with me to Hawaii because flying on a private jet was a whole experience. Noah had already sung its praises to anyone who'd listen, but I hadn't seen the appeal until we all stepped inside one.

"I'm not sure I'm dressed appropriately for this," River said, his shoulder bumping against mine as we settled in our seats.

I stretched out my legs. "I think that's the whole purpose. If you have enough money to fly like this, you can wear anything you want."

"Let's not forget to thank your brother for marrying someone with that kind of money."

"Whoa, let's not go that far. Poor Lior has to put up with Noah, so he's the one we need to thank."

"True." River raised his closed fist, and I bumped it.

Excitement built in my belly as one of the flight attendants closed the plane door. The other came over to us with a tray of drinks.

"Good morning, gentlemen. Would you like a drink? We have champagne, orange juice, or I can get you something from the bar. A cocktail, perhaps?"

"Orange juice for me, please. No one needs to see me drunk before I've had breakfast," I said.

"Understood, sir. Breakfast will be served as soon as we're at cruising altitude." He gave me a glass of orange juice before turning to River. "And you, sir? If you'd like, I can grab our drink menu," he said, his tone carrying a note of flirtation even my straight ass didn't miss.

"Uh, nothing for me, thanks," River stammered, looking away.

"Oh, someone has a new fan," Noah chimed in from across the aisle, his voice laced with mischief. "Guy's clearly into you."

Lex, usually not the instigator but clearly high on love, turned around from the seat in front of us and nudged River playfully. "It's not every day you get hit on at thirty thousand feet."

"We're not there yet." River shot them a bashful look, but something flickered in his eyes—a spark of courage or perhaps just the thrill of the moment. He turned back to the steward, flashing a hesitant but genuine smile. "Actually, a coffee would be nice. Thank you."

"Coming right up," the steward replied, grinning as he moved down the aisle.

I watched the exchange with interest. It was rare to see River being hit on. Especially in the light of day. In a club? Yeah, it had happened a few times, but I had only watched it from afar, unable to make out what was actually being said.

I fiddled with the corner of the in-flight magazine, my mind replaying the last time we had gone out together. We'd laughed, drank, and danced through the evening, sharing the kind of freedom neither of us often experienced.

Being in a relationship had put a stop to most of my partying. Not that I'd done much of it anyway. My brothers, River, and I had a tradition of going to Tanner's on Friday nights, but over the last year, those had been few and far between.

Since my engagement, Lex finding Emery after he'd disappeared due to a car accident that caused him to lose his memory, and then Noah marrying Lior in secret, our schedules hadn't matched, even with us working together.

Then there was River, who put his heart and soul into my parents' restaurant, so trying to pull him away was a feat.

"Remember that night at Haven?" I asked, the words slipping out before I could stop them. "I was like some kind of dude magnet."

River's chuckle was soft. "You always are. People are just drawn to you."

"Guess my gravitational pull doesn't work on flight attendants though." I elbowed him, letting the joke hang between us.

I watched as River's gaze drifted back to the aisle. The steward's smile lingered on him longer, teasing out a flush on his cheeks that hadn't been there before.

Something inside me clenched.

"Hey you think we have to wait long for breakfast? I feel weird."

"Are you sure you're okay?" River's voice was clad with genuine concern. I didn't want to worry him, but how could I explain that I didn't like the way the steward was all flirty with him. I was probably just feeling extra needy with everything that had happened in the last twenty-four hours.

"Yeah, just a weird feeling in my belly."

A moment later, the steward came over holding a tray with a cup of freshly brewed coffee, cream, and sugar. River took the cup and thanked the steward.

"You take it black," he said. "I'll remember that."

"It's not for me," River replied, placing the coffee on the tray in front of me.

I looked at River and then at the steward, whose cheeks suddenly flushed.

"My apologies, sir. Would you like me to bring you a coffee too?"

"I'll wait for breakfast. Thank you."

The steward nodded and then left down the aisle toward the galley.

"You didn't have to give me your coffee," I said.

"I'd like to not see you getting sick when we're going to be stuck in a plane for several hours. Plus, I know what undercaffeinated Adam looks like. Not pretty." He smirked. I would have kicked his leg, but dammit, his gesture and the smell of the coffee grabbed my full attention.

7

———

RIVER

By the time we checked into the hotel, I was more than ready for a shower, a nap, and a drink, and not necessarily in that order.

"How about we drop our stuff off and meet at the bar in half an hour?" Lex called over his shoulder, already heading toward the elevators, holding Emery's hand.

"Make it forty-five," Noah said, winking at his husband.

"Great. I guess it's you and me, buddy, because those four are going to spend the week in their suites," Adam muttered as we walked toward the elevator.

"That's a weird image."

He scoffed. "In their separate suites. Bah, you know what I mean."

I laughed. "I do, but you're cute when you're all bratty." I mimicked his voice in an exaggerated deep tone. "I'm Adam, and I'm upset because my brothers want to hook up with their partners, leaving me all on my—"

He pushed me so hard I almost tripped over his suitcase while laughing.

We were still laughing and messing around when he

47

opened the door to his honeymoon suite, and it dawned on me that it was *the* honeymoon suite.

There were flower petals all over the king-size bed. An ice bucket with a bottle of champagne and a complimentary snack tray with cheese, crackers, and chocolate-covered fruit were arranged on the coffee table.

Adam stood like a statue by the bed, gripping the handle of his suitcase and staring at the arrangement.

"I forgot to tell the hotel," he said, his voice tight as he brought his hand up to his chest and rubbed it.

I dropped my suitcase, walked over to the bed, and picked up each corner of the comforter before bunching it up and dragging the whole thing to the balcony.

I released a sea of flower petals on the guests sunbathing on the loungers near the building.

Sorry for the mess.

Without skipping a beat, I took the comforter back into the room, folded it neatly at the foot of the bed, and turned to Adam. "How about we each grab a shower to freshen up from the flight before we meet the others?"

"Sure."

Adam went first, so while he was out of the room, I looked around and ensured there were no other "gifts" from the hotel for a honeymooning couple.

By the time we got down to the bar, we found Noah and Lior already there, settled comfortably. Noah leaned back against his husband with a roguish grin, and Lior had his arm draped around Noah's shoulders.

"Adam, baby bro!" Noah said, raising his glass in salute. "In the words of the great King Jaffe Joffer, are you going to sew your royal oats this week? It's your honeymoon, after all, and there are plenty of beautiful women here."

"He's sharing a room, remember?" Lex chimed in,

appearing behind us with a smirk on his lips and Emery under his arm.

"Ah, but who says the fun has to be exclusive to the ladies?" Noah's eyes twinkled mischievously. "I mean, no one's saying Adam and River can't have their own kind of fun."

A wave of heat flushed my face at the implication of the word fun, and I caught Noah's gaze. Adam's brothers teasing about the true nature of my friendship with Adam had never affected me before. I mostly ignored their quips because it was all playful joking.

The fact I wished down to my core that it was true played no part because these feelings would only ever be one-sided.

The problem was that with Adam's impending wedding, it had become harder to be close to him, even as a friend. Maybe he hadn't noticed, but his light had dimmed a little since he started his relationship with Victoria.

It had been hard for me to see it happen and not be able to do anything about it.

Now I didn't know anything anymore. The decisions I'd made before the wedding were back on the drawing board because, right now, I needed to be my best friend's best friend, which included making sure he had the time of his life.

"Let's grab those drinks," I said, motioning toward the bartender.

"Good idea," Adam agreed. "I'm in the mood for something alcoholic with an umbrella."

The bartender, a sunkissed man whose shirt clung to his toned chest like a second skin, leaned in with a practiced smile as I approached the bar. "What brings you to paradise?"

"Escaping reality," I replied with a chuckle.

"You've come to the right place," the bartender said. "How can I help you escape?"

Adam cleared his throat. "We'll take two pineapple lychee-tinis," he interjected, claiming the space between the bartender and me with a subtle lean.

I glanced at Adam, but all he offered was a shrug masked by casual indifference.

Did the attention I received unsettle him? And why? He'd never been the possessive type, especially not over random people, even if we were as close as brothers.

"Coming right up," the bartender said, undeterred by Adam's interruption, his smile persisting as he prepared our drinks with a flourish.

I watched the guy's practiced moves with interest. After all, I was in the same industry and was always interested in seeing other people work, but when I glanced back at Adam, his expression was a little tight. Like he was annoyed with something.

"Okay?" I mouthed in his direction.

"Yeah."

The bartender placed the glasses in front of us, taking a little longer to add the garnishes to mine. Okay, even I could accept that it was weird getting attention from two different guys on the same day.

"Thanks," I murmured as we picked up our glasses, my attention briefly caught by the bartender's wink before turning back to Adam.

"Let's find a table," he said, steering us away with a hand on my back. I didn't want to think about what that meant.

"How about we find a table outside? The sun should be setting soon," I suggested, and everyone followed us out.

As we settled into seats overlooking the ocean, I took a long, deep breath, inhaling the salty scent of the sea spray and listening to the sound of waves lapping against the shore.

When was the last time I'd had a real vacation? I couldn't even remember.

I glanced at Adam. He stared at the ocean in front of us, but unlike the rest of the guys sharing loving smiles, his brows were pulled tight together.

"I hate to sound like a broken record…" I started, leaning closer to avoid his brothers listening and butting in.

"I'm okay. Just…thinking," he admitted, his fingers tracing the rim of his glass, causing droplets of condensation to run down.

"About Victoria?" I pressed gently.

He shook his head. "Us. I mean, this—us being here, together." He rushed to clarify.

I reached to place my hand on his arm and squeezed gently. "It's strange, isn't it? How life throws these curveballs."

"More like grenades," he muttered.

We sat in comfortable silence for a moment, the setting sun casting a warm glow over our faces. Adam closed his eyes, giving me the opportunity to drink in the sight of him, bathed in golden light.

"River?" Adam's voice was low, tentative.

"Hmm?"

"Thank you for being here," he said sincerely, reaching across the table to rest his hand near mine. "For everything."

"I'll always have your back, Adam. Always."

It was the coward answer because it was a lie. If Victoria hadn't run, I would have broken my promise.

The clink of glasses and the low hum of conversation enveloped us as we mulled over the glossy brochures Noah had picked up from the reception desk, each promising its own brand of paradise. Adam's fingers brushed against mine as he passed me a pamphlet featuring a snorkeling tour.

"Swimming with turtles, exploring coral reefs, deep-sea fishing…there's certainly a lot to do around here."

Adam smiled while his brothers buzzed with their own excitement, making plans.

"Can you imagine what it'd be like?" Lex asked, leaning back in his chair with a contemplative look. "Us, out there in the big blue, free from everything."

I glanced at Adam again, watching him as he listened to Noah recount a story from his recent honeymoon in Australia. I admired the way his eyes crinkled at the corners when he laughed.

"Hey, River," Noah called out, snapping me back to reality. "You in for the scuba diving? Don't want to miss out on the chance to see some sharks up close."

"Sharks?" My throat tightened around the word. "Definitely. Wouldn't miss it for the world."

Adam snorted and then coughed "Liar" in my direction.

"Good man!" Noah raised his glass.

"Here's to making memories," Lex declared, his eyes sparkling with mischief before he pulled his boyfriend into a quick kiss.

"Memories," I repeated softly, my gaze lingering on Adam once more.

"Cheers" filled the air as we each took a sip.

"All right," Adam said, setting his glass down and meeting my gaze with an earnest intensity. "Let's make this a time we'll never forget."

"Agreed," I replied, my heart pounding with a blend of excitement and trepidation. "What are we doing?"

"Whatever you're doing, you can decide tomorrow because we're out," Lior said, staring intently at Noah.

"Hell yeah, we're out." He stood in a rush and dragged his husband away. "See you at breakfast."

"Those two," Lex said. "I swear they fuck more than bunnies."

Emery chuckled, his face going all red.

"Um…I guess we should probably head off too. Have to unpack and—"

"Have all the sex. Yeah, yeah," Adam said, interrupting Emery.

"We're not…"

It was my turn to laugh. "You totally are."

Emery's face was redder than the wild curls on his head, but he met my eyes and nodded.

With Adam's brothers and their partners gone, we were left on our own to decide what to do for the rest of the evening.

"What do you say about checking out the other bars in this place, roomie?" Adam asked.

I stood and held my fist up for a bump. "Let the bad decisions begin."

8

ADAM

I STOOD at the edge of the wooden dock, my gaze lingering on the sun as it appeared slowly on the horizon.

"Whose idea was this?" Lex said, yawning.

"I believe it was a joint one," Noah added.

"Never. I would never agree to being tortured. I thought this was a vacation," Lex said, pulling Emery closer and hiding his face in his boyfriend's neck, pretending to snore.

"Like it or not, we're here," Lior said. "I, for one, am looking forward to finding out if my husband can provide for me if the end of the world comes and we have nothing more than our natural resources."

"Baby, I could flirt the fish out of any fisherman, but if you're hoping for me to provide in a case of need, you might go hungry."

Lior wrapped his arms around Noah's waist and lifted him over his shoulder. "I guess I'll just have to eat you instead."

I looked away. The sight of both my brothers so perfectly in love made me as happy as it made me sad. While I would never ask them to tone down their affection in front of me, I was also…jealous.

I was supposed to be doing that right now too. Lazy breakfasts in bed, sunscreen application turning into another round of hot sex, talking about the future with a margarita in hand.

Pushing those thoughts away, I glanced at River, who was right beside me, his gaze reflecting the orange hues of the rising sun, a subtle excitement in the tilt of his smile.

"Ready for this?" I asked, half teasing, half serious.

"Yup. Let's see if any of us has improved since we last went fishing with your dad," he replied with a chuckle.

The guide, a seasoned sailor with a weathered look, came out from the boat.

"Good morning, gentlemen. I'm Kianu, and I will be your captain, guide, and, if you're lucky, your chef. I hope you're ready for a good day of fishing. We're forecast for smooth water, so no excuses today. My children's dinner depends on your success."

We all looked at each other, panic setting in everyone's eyes.

Kianu laughed. "Only joking. I don't have kids, and my wife is a vegetarian, but whatever you catch will be your lunch, so I hope you're either very good or brought snacks."

Emery raised his arm, holding a backpack. "Snacks."

"My kind of dude," Kianu said. "All aboard. We've got a pot of coffee to get through while we sail to our destination."

We helped each other onto the rental boat, ready for the safety brief before the start of our adventure and definitely ready for a good cup of coffee.

As the boat sailed farther into the Pacific, I took note of the light of the rising sun on the island's shore. It was truly a beautiful sight.

Kianu delivered on his promise. The coffee was good, and

he even threw in a batch of pineapple-shaped shortbread cookies made by his wife.

By the time we arrived at our destination, the sun was high in the sky and we could no longer see land.

River sat across from me, preparing his line as Kianu instructed. The reels were bigger and heavier than the ones we'd used to fish at the lake in Stillwater with my dad.

While I struggled to set mine up, River seemed like he'd been doing it for years. My gaze was fixed on his capable hands and the way the muscles in his forearms moved. He had corded muscles going all the way up to where his tattoos disappeared under the sleeves of his T-shirt.

"Adam? You all right there?" Lex's voice pulled me from my thoughts.

"Yeah, just…I don't think this is an activity I'll excel at."

"Here. I'll set yours up for you," River said, placing his rod beside him and taking mine.

The boat bobbed gently on the undulating waves, and I found myself staring again at River's hands as he worked. When I looked up at his face, he was smiling to himself. His tongue peeked out a little from between his lips. He was so focused on the task that he didn't even notice, which made me smile because it brought back memories of when we were kids playing or trying to figure out the rules of a game and River would do the same thing.

When both our reels were set up, we cast our lines into the water.

My fingers wrapped around the fishing rod with faux confidence. Mostly, I hoped I wouldn't get a bite because the fish would probably pull me out of the boat and into the sea, where I'd get eaten alive.

"All right, guys," Noah declared, "let's see who can catch the biggest fish! Loser buys drinks at karaoke tonight!"

Lex whooped, his competitive spark igniting instantly,

and Lior shot me a grin while keeping a protective arm around Noah. Probably in case he decided to catch a shark with his bare hands.

"May the best angler win," River said.

The ocean stretched before us, a vast unknown full of possibility and hidden currents. "Deal!" I replied. Fake it 'til you make it, right? "I'm going to claim that title. Get ready for the tales of my legendary catch!"

"Legendary?" Lex's voice cut through the sound of the waves slapping against the hull. "Please, Adam! Remember that fishing trip we took with Dad when we were fifteen? You nearly fell out of the boat over that tiny fish!"

I punched River's arm as he laughed so hard he nearly fell off his seat before I focused back on my reel, willing it to bring me a good one.

For a while, all I could hear was the sound of the waves and a seagull or two in the distance. I lost myself in thoughts, but for once, it wasn't my failed relationship, the embarrassment of being jilted just before the wedding, or the bill I'd been left with.

As my hands gripped the reel, I glanced around at my family, and all I could feel was peace. The sun warmed my face so I closed my eyes, seeing the bright orange through my eyelids.

We were still at the beginning of the vacation, but I already knew it had been a good idea to bring everyone along. In their individual ways, they were all helping me feel a little more like myself. And even though I was still very emotionally sore from what happened only days ago, I was also starting to see where I'd lost myself a little to my relationship with Victoria.

Something pulled on my rod. "Can you guys feel that?" I asked, more to myself than anyone else, as I sensed the subtle pull beneath the surface. "Guys, I think I've got a bite!" The shout left my lips before I processed the tingle of excitement rushing up the rod.

My heart thumped erratically as I tried to reel in whatever was caught on the line. "It must be huge." I declared, more out of hope than certainty, gripping the rod with all my strength.

"Come on, Adam," River encouraged. "You've got this."

My arms ached as I gave a final tug, and with a splash that sprayed cold droplets across my face, a small fish landed on the deck. It flopped pitifully, its scales catching the sunlight.

"Look at this beauty!" I held it up high, filled with pride.

The moment of cheers gave into an eruption of laughter.

"That's dinner sorted," Noah said.

"We're gonna need a big fire for that," Lex added.

"Hey, I'm not seeing your big catches," River said, coming to my defense. He didn't need to because I wasn't taking my brothers' ribbing seriously, but I liked that he did.

Kianu surfaced from the cabin with a camera.

"Okay, guys. Time to pose. You're going on my wall."

They all gathered around me and the fish, and at Kianu's signal, everyone shouted "Fishy!" as he took the photo.

"What are you going to do with it?" River asked.

"I have to release him. No way I could stand to eat him. Look at his face." I turned the fish's head to face River, and his face turned a little green.

"Yeah. Agreed."

"Well, it's a good thing I have a feast for you, and that I was joking when I said you'd eat what you caught. Reel everything in, and let's celebrate our catch and release in style," Kianu said.

As we reeled in our lines, Kianu brought a tray filled with sandwiches. Then he returned downstairs, coming back up with a six-pack of beer.

"I'm afraid this is all I allow on the boat," he said, "but a celebration is in order."

I chuckled. "What do you do when someone catches an actual big fish? Throw fireworks?"

He flipped the lid on a can of soda and took a swig. "You'd be surprised at how little fishing actually happens on these trips. Most people just want to go out in open water and maybe swim a little."

"You mean we can swim out here?" River asked.

"Sure, you can."

Before Kianu had finished, River's T-shirt was over his head. He ran toward the back of the boat and threw himself into the water.

I followed him to see him resurface.

"Guys, the water is phenomenal. Jump in before you eat."

I looked back at the guys who'd started taking their shirts off. Kianu sat on the cushioned bench and flipped his backward cap forward before leaning back, looking as chill as anything.

"I guess this makes me the winner because with you all splashing around, you're going to scare all the fish," I said, throwing my T-shirt onto the pile and jumping into the water after everyone.

"This was the best idea ever," Lex said.

"I believe your exact words were—" Emery started but was cut off by Lex, who kissed him.

A quick glance at Noah and Lior revealed they were also whispering to each other between sweet kisses.

I looked away, feeling like an intruder in their moments.

"You can say something, you know?"

I turned to River. "What do you mean?"

"If it's hard for you to see them all loved-up, you can ask them to tone it down. They'd do it in a heartbeat."

"I know, but I don't want to do that to them. They're so in love. It's nice to see. Even if it didn't happen for me, I like that it happened for them. They both deserve to be really happy."

River stared at me, his green eyes framed by long eyelashes glistening with water droplets. He came closer until I felt his hand take mine under the water.

"It's going to happen for you too, Adam."

A lump formed in my throat, but I didn't want to give in to thoughts that had no place on a happy day.

"Of course it will," I said, grinning. "I'm already the best fisherman. It can only get better from here on."

9

———

RIVER

THE FRISBEE SLICED through the humid air. I watched Adam's lean form as he darted across the sand to catch it. Adam was all tousled hair, defined muscles, and a smile that went on for days.

His arms flexed as he threw the Frisbee back in my direction.

I jumped to catch it, feeling the grains of sand shift under my feet.

"Hey, look at you!" I teased, nudging him playfully when he returned to my side. "You've taken to vacation life like a fish to water. You know, like that lucky fish you caught yesterday."

Adam chuckled. "What can I say? Maybe it's the company." He winked and threw himself on his beach towel.

I followed him, dropping the plastic disk on the sand.

"I am a joy to be around," I joked.

Adam lay sideways and rested his head on his hand. "I missed this, you know. Doing nothing, being with you, listening to music." He sighed and reached into his bag to grab his iPod.

63

"You do know phones do that these days, right?" I teased.

"I know. But they're also attention whores, and when I want to chill with our playlists, I don't want the world interrupting."

I smiled as he passed one of the earbuds to me. For as long as I could remember, we'd made playlists for each other. I started it when we were bored one particular summer, and when he'd been gifted an iPod for his birthday, we took it to a new level. We had a playlist for every mood, and I loved it.

For a while, we lay there under the late afternoon sun, listening to a nineties summer playlist.

My belly rumbled, so I turned to him. "Want to grab some food?"

"Absolutely. I was right when I said we wouldn't see the happy couples for the rest of the day," he said, pulling his phone out of his bag. "I guess we're on our own for dinner."

"They did say couples massages always put them in the mood."

"Like they ever have a problem with that."

I snorted. There was no arguing that.

We picked up our stuff and walked side by side toward the beachfront restaurant, the sand giving way beneath our feet.

"Look at that," Adam murmured, nodding toward the horizon where the sunset painted the sky with beautiful hues of gold and amber. "Doesn't it make you want to just…stay here forever?"

"Sometimes," I confessed. "But life's waiting for us back home, isn't it?"

"Is it?" he pondered aloud. "Or are we just afraid to find out what could be if we took the leap?"

I glanced at him, at the earnestness etched into his features, and the weight of my secret pressed down on me with renewed force. What would happen if I took that leap? If I dared to voice my truth?

"Maybe," I said, the word hanging between us.

The restaurant buzzed with life, the evening crowd a blend of tourists and locals. We found a cozy table outside on the patio facing the ocean and sat down.

The server didn't take long to give us a menu and take our drink order.

"I'm impressed by the service here. If the food is as good, I think I've found my favorite place on this island," I said.

A girl at a nearby table angled her chair to face us, her gaze locked on Adam with an eagerness that set my stomach in knots. "Hey there! I was wondering if you know what's good to eat in this place," she asked, but her body language told me the last thing on her mind was food.

I felt my jaw clench, a wave of unease rising in me. I wanted to shield Adam from her, to claim his attention as solely mine. But I held back. It wasn't my place.

"It's our first time here," Adam responded with kindness, never crossing into flirtation, his focus flickering back to me.

"It's my first time here too. In Maui, I mean. It was meant to be a girls' vacation, but my friend got sick, and I didn't want all our plans to go to waste."

"Um…I'm really sorry to hear about your friend," Adam said. "I'm sure it's not as fun traveling on your own."

The girl shrugged. "As they say, a stranger is a friend you haven't met yet." She leaned closer. "There are some strangers here I wouldn't mind getting to know better."

"Just as long as they're not serial killers." His gaze flickered to me again, and I clung to the fact he didn't seem interested in the girl in the slightest.

The girl giggled, a sound that seemed to resonate at a frequency designed to grab attention. Her hair, a cascade of sunkissed waves, was tossed with calculated carelessness. "You don't look like a serial killer."

It was Adam's turn to shrug. "Vacation wardrobe."

"I can't tell if you're serious or joking," she said.

At that time, the server returned to take our order, and while she listed the day's specials, the girl made her way inside the restaurant.

"She was very interested," I said after the server left us. "What was it that Noah said? You could be *sewing your royal oats* before the main course."

He laughed. "Aside from the fact I'm here with my best friend, who I wouldn't ditch for any girl, I'm also not interested in hooking up or vacation flings."

"It's too early. I get it."

He gazed out at the beach in front of us. "It's more than that. I'm not sure I'll ever trust again, and it's not just trusting someone else. It's trusting myself."

I squeezed his shoulder. As much as I wanted to tell him the right person was out there and all that, I didn't want to play down his feelings. He was entitled to feel like not touching another person ever again. He was entitled to feel bitter, sad, and angry. It was all part of the healing process.

Yeah, you know all about that, don't you, River?

The food was even better than the service, and after chatting with the server, we were given a brief tour of the kitchen. We met the chef, a local woman who'd learned to cook from her grandmother and had a no-nonsense approach to handling a kitchen. She was a hoot and made us promise to come back with Adam's brothers and their partners.

As night draped over us, we retreated to our hotel room. Our conversation flowed easily, so despite our skin itching from the sea salt, we grabbed drinks from the mini bar and sat on the balcony.

"River, you know, today…it was good. Really good," Adam said.

"Good days are what we're here for, right?" He raised his can of soda, and I met it with mine.

When we finished our drinks, we took turns in the shower and settled in bed. The soft glow of the bedside lamp cast a muted light across the room, illuminating the space just enough for me to make out Adam's silhouette.

"Remember that time you stole the keys for Lusitana from your parents so I could use the kitchen?" I asked.

Adam chuckled, the sound rich with nostalgia. "How could I forget? I was grounded for a month for pulling that stunt."

"But that roast pork was to die for."

"Totally worth it. I still don't know why you didn't become a chef."

I smiled to myself, recalling the surge of triumph followed by the blue lights of the police coming into the kitchen because a neighbor thought the restaurant was being burgled. "I love cooking, but I think doing it for a living would take the fun out of it. Managing the restaurant allows me to have fun in the kitchen when they need me, but I also get to do other things, like working on customer experience and building relationships with long-standing customers."

"And making sure Lusitana will still stand in place in thirty years."

I laughed. "And that."

As the night deepened and our anecdotes dwindled to murmurs, a silence settled between us.

"I know I've already said it, but thanks for being here, River," Adam whispered across the dimness, his voice a tender caress against the room's stillness.

I turned my head to meet his gaze, finding his blue eyes

earnest and open, a universe of gratitude and trust within them.

"I wouldn't be anywhere else," I whispered back, even though the devil on my shoulder called me a liar.

Eventually, the exhaustion of the day caught up to me. As I teetered on the edge of sleep, my mind conjured images of our day together. Just Adam and River.

Even as my heart craved more, I felt grateful that I'd had this time with him.

With one last glance at his silhouette, barely discernible in the moonlight that filtered through the blinds, I let sleep claim me.

10

———

ADAM

As consciousness crept in gently, I opened my eyes slowly, still trying to decide whether I was looking forward to the day or if I wanted to pretend to be asleep for the next week.

The familiar weight of another body beside me tugged at the edges of my drowsy mind. I turned my head to the sleepy figure and smiled.

River's chest rose and fell with the serene rhythm of undisturbed sleep, allowing me a moment to watch his peaceful form.

I traced the line of his spine with my gaze, from the broad shoulders descending to the unexpected fullness of his ass beneath the sheet.

A subtle heat prickled my skin.

Sure, I'd seen him almost naked plenty of times. Apart from all the vacations we'd had together, including this one, we'd shared a room in college before we moved into an apartment with my brothers.

River walking into the kitchen in the morning, half-asleep, going straight to the coffee maker had been a daily occurrence. I'd caught him enough times that I'd stopped teasing him about his morning wood showing through his boxer shorts and just gotten used to the daily salute.

Sunlight painted River in warmth, showcasing his tattoos like a work of art.

Molecular structures spiraled all along his arms and across his back. I recognized the coffee molecule. His first tattoo, which he said represented his first true love.

He'd gained more tattoos over the years. Some I vaguely remembered the meaning of. Others were new. I wondered when he'd gotten them done.

On his calf, among the scientific renderings, bloomed edible flowers, showcasing his passions for food, service, and beauty.

In that quiet moment, my heart swelled with something I couldn't name.

A week ago, if anyone had told me I'd be sharing a bed with River, I'd have laughed. If Victoria had been present, she'd have stomped out.

I'd known River for so long that he was an automatic part of my life. A constant, like breathing. I'd never felt embarrassed about seeing him undress and didn't have a problem getting undressed in front of him. I didn't care that he was gay, and it never occurred to me that, as a man, I could be the kind of guy he was attracted to.

If I was, he'd never let it show.

My intrusive thoughts were broken when a soft sigh escaped River's lips. I held my breath, afraid to disturb him.

Or afraid to get caught.

River shifted, a quiet inhale followed by a less quiet exhale. My heart stuttered, and I snapped my eyes shut, pretending to be asleep.

Once I was sure he was still asleep, I slid from the

warmth of the sheets and made my way to the bathroom, locking the door behind me.

I leaned against the wooden door, taking a moment to gather myself.

What was I doing staring at my friend's almost-naked body? Even more confusing was that I wasn't just morning wood hard. I was need-to-get-off-right-now hard.

Stripping off my clothes, I stepped into the shower, not waiting for the water to warm up. The cold spray of the water, a stark contrast to the heat pooled in my belly, offered only temporary relief.

I pressed my forehead against the cool tile. The water sluiced over me but couldn't wash away the images etched into my mind. The curves of River's body bathed in morning light, the tattoos that etched his history across his skin, the peace that radiated from him as he slept, unaware of my tumultuous thoughts.

What was this pull I suddenly felt toward my best friend? Was it the shock of Victoria's departure that made me reach for something familiar, the time we spent together yesterday, or was it something that had always been there, under my skin, waiting to be released?

I pressed more of my upper body against the cool tiles, seeking support for my trembling legs. My hand made its way across my chest, trailing lower, driven by a compulsion I couldn't control.

Each stroke of my cock was powered by the unexplainable need to get off. I hadn't had sex in weeks, and with the stress of the wedding, I'd been too tired to jerk off.

That was it. I just needed to get off, and everything would go back to normal.

With my eyes sealed shut, I surrendered to the fantasy. River's laugh, warm and genuine, rang in my ears, intertwining with the sound of the falling water. I could almost feel the press of his body against mine, solid and real.

"River…" I moaned, his name falling from my lips as my pace quickened, chasing a release that scratched just under my skin.

Each breath came sharper than the last, punctuated by the rhythm I set against my own skin, desperately imagining it was my best friend guiding me to the edge.

In the steam-filled shower, where the world beyond the glass doors ceased to exist, I allowed myself this transgression. One I couldn't name or comprehend, but it just felt so damned good, I couldn't bring myself to resist.

The buildup of pleasure approached, relentless and consuming, as my breath hitched in my throat. My hand moved faster and faster until the tingling sensation in my balls built up to my spine. The elusive bliss that had hovered just out of reach was now within my grasp.

My thoughts swirled with the image of River, his smile, those almost-translucent eyes that mirrored the passion for all the things he loved.

With my mind filled with thoughts of my best friend, I came so hard I had to lock my knees so I wouldn't slip down.

"Adam?" River's voice pierced through the veil of steam, shattering the moment. My hand stilled, my eyes flying open to the clinical white bathroom tiles as I watched my release running down the drain. All evidence washed away. I stood there, water still cascading down my back, my heart thundering against my ribs.

"Y-Yeah?" I croaked, the word barely carrying over the sound of the shower.

"Everything okay?"

"Fine, just…dropped the soap." The lie was clumsy. If I'd told him I was jerking off, he wouldn't have thought anything of it, but with the realization of what I'd done hitting me, I couldn't bring myself to even joke about it.

With trembling hands, I turned off the water, the sudden silence leaving room for my errant thoughts. Why River? Why now? The questions pummeled my conscience, each one a reminder of the line I'd unwittingly crossed.

"Lex asked if we're meeting them for breakfast. They want to hit the beach before it gets too hot."

I got out of the shower, avoiding looking at my reflection in the mirror.

"Sure. I'll be right out."

"Can you hurry up? Gotta take a leak," River said, oblivious to my betrayal of our friendship.

Clutching a towel from the rack, I wrapped it securely around my waist, the fabric clinging to the dampness of my skin.

Stepping into the bedroom, I almost ran into River, who practically pushed me out of the way to get into the bathroom. At least that gave me some precious minutes to get my head straight.

"What were you doing in here that took you so long? Jerking off?" he asked from behind the door.

"What do you think? It's my honeymoon, after all."

My comment was met with silence until I heard the sound of the shower running.

I got dressed in my swim trunks and a T-shirt and went over to the balcony. Maybe fresh ocean air was what I needed to reset.

A large group of people took over a row of sun loungers by the pool. I tried to take my mind off what I'd done by people-watching, but then my gaze locked in on one of the couples in the group. Two guys sat facing each other on a lounger.

They were smiling and talking, and occasionally, they'd

touch each other's hands. I couldn't tell if they were friends or more.

When someone brought them over their drinks, they toasted and then shared a short kiss.

I couldn't look away even if I felt like I was intruding on their moment.

"You need to get a grip, Adam," I muttered to myself as I sat on a chair facing away from the group.

"Hey," River said, coming out to join me after a while. His voice was bright and happy like he was ready to face the day and have fun.

Fun.

I'd had some of that already.

"Ready to go down?" he asked.

"Huh."

"For breakfast. Are you okay? You look flushed." He pressed a hand against my forehead, but I pushed it off.

"I'm fine. It's too hot out already, that's all. Let's go."

I couldn't tell if he could sense my unease, but I was acutely aware of the space where our friendship ended and this new, confusing territory began. A line had been crossed, even if only in my mind, and now I stood on unfamiliar ground.

"Ladies, gents, and enbies, let's welcome our new grooms!" Noah teased as we sat at the breakfast table.

"You're not even half as funny as you think you are," I said, grabbing the pot of coffee from the center of the table.

"Are you saying you aren't following the honeymoon ritual of making sweet loooove all night?" Lex added. "Even after we left you alone all day yesterday?"

"Not you too," I said, rolling my eyes. I picked up the menu and scanned through the omelet options.

"Good morning, gentlemen. I'm Morgan, and I'm here

to take your breakfast orders if you'd like anything from the menu."

I looked up to find myself staring at the bartender from our first night at the resort.

"You're the bartender," River said, smiling at the guy.

My gut twisted and I lost the appetite I had. "I'll just go hit the buffet." I pushed away from the table and went searching for carbs. Pilling up eggs, ham, croissants, and chocolate spread, I didn't return to the table until the guy was gone.

"He's really nice," Emery said.

"You'd say that, baby. He agreed to serve you pancakes with ice cream for breakfast," Lex added.

"Seriously though, the guy is hot, and he seems to have a soft spot for River," Noah said.

"I don't think so," River said, and the twist in my belly eased a little.

"What's the plan for today? Beach and then what? Are we swimming with the sharks or the turtles?" I asked, grabbing a croissant and stuffing it in my mouth.

Food, coffee, and some kind of physical activity. That's what I needed.

"I was actually joking about the sharks," Noah said. "There's only one set of teeth I want on my skin, and it's sitting at this table."

Lior ran his hand over his face in a clear sign of resignation, but the corners of his lips raised a little as he looked at my brother.

Damn, what would it feel to have that kind of love? The one where you can be totally deranged like my brother, and instead of being put down for it, your partner finds you amusing and adorable.

I glanced at River, who looked from Noah to me and wiggled his brows.

11

RIVER

"You are going down." I watched Adam hurl a handful of water at Lex, his matching blue eyes sparkling as he dunked his twin brother under the water.

"Come on, River! Save me from this maniac!" Lex hollered between breaths, dashing behind me as if I could shield him from Adam's playful wrath when teamed up with Emery.

Adam's chuckle rippled through the air, warm and infectious. I couldn't help but join in, scooping water in my palms and pouring it over Lex's head, much to his mock indignation.

"Traitor!"

"Hey, just protecting my own interests."

We messed around in the water until my fingers were like prunes. It reminded me of when Adam's parents would rent a cabin by the lake in Stillwater and take me along on their family vacation. Me and the guys would practically spend the whole time in the water, coming out only when their mom called us in with promises of her amazing food.

It was on one of those vacations that I'd asked Jack if I

could work at the restaurant. I'd always been fascinated by the way Jack ran the restaurant and how much it was part of the fabric of the Spencer family. Being an only child to a single parent, I'd craved being part of something like that. Something bigger that was also part of the community.

Speaking of which, I was due a call to my mom. A few years ago, she left her nursing job to do contract work abroad because she wanted to travel more now that I was an adult.

We had a great relationship, but I wouldn't say we were super close. As a single mom, she'd worked all the hours she could get at the hospital, which meant I'd spent my time with Adam and his family or at home alone.

I loved my mom, but I certainly couldn't say our relationship had the same level of connection as the Spencer parents and their sons.

Still, I missed her, and it had been a while since I'd received a postcard from her, so I should check in and see how the South of France was treating her.

"River, you coming?" Lex called out. He was already heading back to the beach to join Noah and Lior, who'd gone back earlier.

"Be right there," I responded, glancing at Adam. He was gazing out toward the horizon. I couldn't blame him for being more introspective than usual, but I knew there would always be a part of me that wanted to fix things for him.

"Race you back," Adam said, splashing water in my direction.

"Bring it on," I shot back. I was nothing if not competitive. Hey, I worked in the restaurant business. Competitive was my middle name. Besides, he already had the best fisherman title.

We joined the others just as Noah emerged from the resort's thatched bar, a tray of vividly hued cocktails balanced expertly in his hands. I watched him weave through clusters of beachgoers like a pro.

"Here comes the liquid sunshine!" Noah announced.

"About time, dude," Lex teased, reaching for a glass garnished with a slice of pineapple and a tiny umbrella.

"Cheers to another day in paradise," Noah said, lifting his cocktail high before taking a long sip.

"Paradise indeed," Adam echoed.

"Speaking of paradise," Noah continued, settling into the lounger already taken by Lior and leaning back. Lior wrapped his arms around Noah, kissing his shoulder. "I've been thinking. We should make a thing of this."

"Of what?" Lex asked.

"Just us. Chilling and hanging out. Our very own annual bro-cation."

"Dude, I already see you every day," Adam said, and Noah threw the little umbrella from his drink at his brother.

Lex leaned forward on his lounger, resting his elbows on his knees. "Noah has a point. Spencer Brothers PR is more than just a business. It's more than the next big project or making a name for ourselves."

"True," Adam mused, sipping his drink through the straw. "It's about family. Keeping this connection strong, no matter how busy we get."

"Exactly," Noah agreed. "It's why we started this whole venture. To build something of our own, something as big as Lusitana that is just ours."

"Plus, these getaways give us the chance to unwind and enjoy what our hard work can afford us," Lex added, reclining beside Emery with a contented sigh.

"Here's to traditions," I toasted, raising my glass toward the brothers, each so different, yet every single one a Spencer through and through.

"Here's to traditions," they echoed.

The laughter and conversation flowed as freely as the drinks, and I couldn't help but feel a surge of appreciation for these moments.

"Speaking of success," Noah began, turning toward me with a relaxed grin, the fading light catching the glint in his eyes. "How's Lusitana holding up? Last I heard, you guys were booked solid for months."

"Actually, it's never been better," I replied, my chest swelling with a quiet pride that I rarely allowed myself to acknowledge. "We're experimenting with new flavors, fusing traditional dishes with modern twists but staying true to your family's Portuguese roots. People seem to love it."

"And you've got that farm-to-table thing going on too, right?" Lex chimed in. "Eco-friendly and gourmet—talk about hitting the jackpot."

"Something like that." A smile crept onto my lips as I thought about the restaurant, my sanctuary. To pour passion into cuisine, to watch strangers unite over a dining experience I helped create—it was more than just work. It was sharing a piece of myself, an act of service that connected me to this family, to Adam.

"Hey, you know what you need, River?" Lex asked with a mischievous wink. "A good hookup to celebrate your achievements. How about that bartender Morgan? He's been eyeing you every time we drop by for drinks."

Adam's chuckle joined Lex's teasing, but I could sense an undercurrent of something else in his tone. "Yeah, Morgan's not bad-looking. What do you say, Riv?"

Not this again.

"Guys, come on," I tried to laugh it off, though I couldn't quite meet Adam's gaze. "I'm pretty happy with how things are at the moment."

"Sure, sure," Lex drawled, unconvinced, but he let it slide, turning back to finish his cocktail with a satisfied slurp.

Adam's eyes lingered on me a second longer, searching, before he also redirected his attention to the horizon.

"I'm going for a short walk before getting ready for dinner. My ass is numb from sitting here all this time," I said.

Sand clung to my feet as I walked, the waves kissing my feet every time they came up the shore.

Relief washed over me as I walked, yet a weight lingered on my chest. One I'd been shouldering for far too long. My feelings for Adam were like the molecular structures tattooed on my arms—intricate, complex, and bonded by invisible forces.

Some days, the secrets I carried felt too heavy a burden. Now, as I gazed at the expanse of water beside me, I wondered if I could share at least one of those secrets. I'd always been too afraid in case Adam made assumptions that were way too close to the truth, but it also meant I wasn't being my authentic self with the one person who knew more about me than anyone else.

"River. Wait."

"Adam," I replied. "What are you doing here?"

"I wanted to apologize for Lex and Noah back there," he began, his tone sincere. "They don't know when to stop sometimes."

"Nothing to apologize for," I managed. "It's just…their timing wasn't great."

"Timing?" he echoed, stepping closer, his gaze never leaving mine.

"Never mind," I said, looking down at my feet, suddenly finding the patterns in the sand fascinating.

"River," he said softly, moving to stand beside me, watching the waves roll in. "You're always there for me, for everyone else. Let me in. Sometimes, it feels like there's this barrier between us. I can't see it, but I can feel it."

"Sometimes questions are better left unasked."

"Maybe," Adam repeated, quieter this time. "Or maybe we're just afraid of the answers."

I glanced up at him then, caught off guard by the intensity of his gaze, by the raw honesty I saw.

"Come on," he said after a moment. "Let's head back before Lex drinks all the good stuff."

"Right. Can't let that happen."

We started back together, the silence between us stretching out like the infinite ocean in front of us.

"River," he began, "why don't you date much? I mean, you're a great guy, and it's not like you lack offers."

I'd give it to him. His timing was impeccable because as much as I wanted to cling to the layers of self-preservation, there was also part of me that needed to know how Adam would react.

"It's complicated."

"Complicated how?" There was that gentle probing again, laced with genuine concern, and I knew there was no more evading the truth.

Taking a deep breath, I let the words tumble out. "I'm demisexual. I don't...I can't feel attraction to someone unless there's an emotional bond first. A real connection."

My confession hung in the air. For a moment, he said nothing, and that silence was louder than any reaction I had braced for. Then he nodded slowly, like he was processing this sliver of my identity I'd just laid bare before him.

"Demisexual," he repeated, testing the word. "So, all those times people flirted with you..."

"Meant nothing," I finished for him. "They were just faces, Adam. No matter how attractive or interested they were, without that connection, it's like trying to admire a view with the curtains closed."

"River," Adam murmured, his voice carrying a note of

awe mingled with something else—something deeper. "That's…honestly, that's really brave of you to share."

My shoulders, which I hadn't noticed had been tense, relaxed slightly. The fear of being misunderstood, judged even, ebbed away with the tide.

"Is that why…?" He trailed off, uncertainty flickering in his gaze.

"Is that why what?" I prompted, even though I was terrified he was about to voice my biggest fear in coming out to him.

"Nothing," he said quickly, shaking his head. But the curiosity lingered, filled with unspoken questions.

"Adam," I started, "there's a lot you don't know about me. Things I never thought I could tell anyone, especially you."

"Especially me?" His voice held a tremor, a hint of vulnerability that matched mine.

"Because you matter more to me than anyone else," I admitted, my voice breaking. "You always have."

Under the darkening sky, our gazes locked again, and I wondered if he could see the truth I'd kept hidden for so long.

"Does it change things?" I asked, bracing myself for the impact of his answer, as terrifying as it was.

"No," he said earnestly. "It doesn't change how I see you. If anything, it makes me…respect you more." His gaze held mine, unflinching and sincere.

"Respect me?"

"Of course. You're true to yourself, even when it's hard. That takes courage."

Right there, on a beach, thousands of miles away from our reality, I saw something shift in Adam's blue eyes, as if he were seeing me fully for the first time.

"Tell me more," he said, demonstrating his usual hunger for knowledge.

I hesitated, keenly aware of the magnitude of this moment. "There's not much to tell," I confessed. "It took me a long time to figure out why I'd find someone attractive or interesting but have no desire to be intimate with them. I thought I was broken or…" Just irrevocably in love with my best friend since that kiss when we were fourteen. A kiss Adam had never brought up since.

I'd confessed one truth tonight already. I was not prepared to admit another.

That one would definitely mark the end of my friendship with Adam.

12

—

ADAM

Back in the coolness of the room, River headed straight for the shower. I couldn't blame him for seeking a moment on his own after I'd practically pried his secret out of him.

I wasn't yet sure how I felt about it. Part of me wondered if I should be hurt that my best friend had hidden a part of himself from me for so long. But considering I was also harboring my own secret, I understood that sometimes telling the truth wasn't an option because we had more to lose than to gain.

I mean, what would I gain from telling River I was starting to find him fascinating in a way I'd never considered before and that I wasn't sure it wasn't just some kind of trauma-induced thing.

As I riffled through my suitcase for a shirt to wear for dinner, I found my empty sunglasses case. I raised my hand to my head, only to come away empty-handed. Of course I'd lose the new pair I'd bought for the honeymoon after Victoria complained my old sunglasses looked like they'd gone to high school with me.

She'd been right, but if something wasn't broken, why fix

85

it? I'd given in and bought a new pair I planned to keep for the next thirty years.

"Hey, I forgot my sunglasses on the beach," I called out to River. "I'm going to see if I can find them."

"Okay," he shouted back.

I spared a glance toward the bathroom, willing my brain to give me a break from all the thoughts I didn't need to be having. I was supposed to be crying over the end of my almost marriage. Feeling sorry for myself for being dumped. *Not* wondering about a naked River only a few feet away.

As I turned the corner of the hallway outside my room, I almost collided with my brother.

"Hey, I was coming to see you," Lex said. "Were you looking for these, by any chance?" He held up my sunglasses.

"Fuck, yeah. I thought I'd lost them."

"You left them behind when you ran over to River like he'd taken all your toys and run away."

"Yeah, I was…" I trailed off, avoiding meeting Lex's probing gaze.

"Hey. Talk to me. Do you remember what you did when Emery disappeared?"

"I went to your place and stalked his social media to find answers about where he was?"

The pain in Lex's eyes always got to me when he talked about the year he thought he'd lost Emery when, in fact, he'd been in an accident and had lost his memory. His mom had manipulated him into going back home by hiding his old life from him, and it wasn't until Lex and Emery were acciden-tally set up by Emery's friend Ellie that they reconnected and fell in love all over again.

"No, Adam. You came to my place and stayed with me. You kept me company, and yes, you tried to figure out what had happened to Emery, but for me, the most important thing was that you were there for me. I wouldn't have wanted anyone else. I know you have River, but I hope you know I'm here for you, right?"

I exhaled. "I know, Lex. You have no idea how much I appreciate that everyone is here with me. It's like…I feel like I can't trust my feelings anymore," I confessed, the words tumbling out in a rush. "Ever since Victoria, everything's upside down, and now—" I choked on the rest, the truth too raw, too new.

Lex's expression changed. "Has something else happened? Has Victoria been in touch or…shit, is she leaving you to foot the whole bill for a wedding that didn't happen?"

I played with the arms of my sunglasses. "It doesn't have anything to do with Victoria. I mean, I don't think it does, but I don't know. I…something's changed, and I don't know if it was always there or triggered by her. I don't trust myself anymore."

"Adam, whatever you're feeling, it's okay. You're allowed to be confused."

"Am I?" I asked, not bothering to hide my skepticism. But Lex's words were reassuring. Something in me might be longing for something, someone, it shouldn't, and maybe I didn't understand it, but I could take my time to figure it out. "Thank you, Lex."

"Anytime, big brother," Lex said, pulling me into a tight hug. Something about being this close to my twin brother always made me feel safe, like there was nothing more right in my life.

"I guess I should go back to my room." I nodded toward the other end of the hallway. "River is probably done with his shower, so I'll jump in quickly so we can get to dinner on time. I'm craving a good steak and a bottomless beer."

"Now there's an idea," Lex agreed. "I'll meet you at the restaurant in a bit."

The door to the room clicked shut behind me, and I was

met with silence before soft, rhythmic moans breached the quiet. They came from the bathroom, muffled by water spray but unmistakable. Heat flushed through my body as my hand froze on the back of the door.

River.

My heart thudded, and I swallowed hard, my tongue too big inside my mouth. I should go back outside, give him a few more minutes, and then come back in and pretend I didn't know what was happening behind the closed door of our shared bathroom.

I should. But my feet were glued to the spot on the cold marble floor.

River was always so composed, so gentle in his mannerisms. Hearing him like this, unguarded and gasping, was like opening a new window into my best friend.

"Ah…" River's voice cracked slightly, edged with pleasure.

I pressed my back against the door, my eyes fluttering closed as the sounds lured me further into a maze of desire I'd never felt pulled into exploring. This was River—my best friend, the boy who spent so much time at my place that he had half my closet space filled with his clothes. The friend who'd listened to me every time I got my heart broken. The man I was suddenly feeling conflicted about.

Curiosity mingled with arousal, igniting a fire in my veins. Curiosity about what River might look like in that moment of abandon, about the fantasies and the images in his head as he touched himself.

And curiosity about myself, about the flickering flame inside that seemed to grow brighter with every stifled moan that slipped through the cracks.

I shifted, the movement stirring the air around me. My body responded, betraying me with a tent in my swim trunks.

"Fuck." Another moan slipped through the bathroom door.

"River," I whispered, the name a prayer on my lips for the second time today.

What did it mean to feel this pull, this yearning for someone who had always been a constant, platonic presence in my life?

Why now? Why a man? Why River?

I leaned back and slid down to the floor, knees drawn up, head resting against the door.

The moans softened then, tapering into silence, leaving me alone with the pounding of my pulse and the questions swirling in my head.

Then, River's voice shattered the quietude, his climax arriving with my name torn from his lips. "Adam!"

My heart lurched against my ribcage. My name sounded different when carried on the wave of River's release.

The room suddenly seemed smaller, the air charged with the electricity.

"Dammit," I cursed under my breath. I pushed myself up from the floor. My unsteady legs made it harder to move, but the need to escape the confines of the room propelled me forward. I reached for the door handle, my hand trembling as I turned it.

The hall outside offered no relief. I paced between the two walls, which now felt like they were closing in on me. I pressed the heels of my palms into my eyes, trying to physically push away the intensity of what I'd heard, what I felt.

I wanted to shout at myself to get it together, but how could I when my world had just tilted on its axis?

With each inhale of my breath, I tried to steady my heartbeat, to cool the flush that had spread across my cheeks.

I needed space and time to understand why hearing my

name fall from River's lips had felt like a call to something deeper, something real. And terrifying.

Why had he called my name? Did it mean he felt a connection with me? When he explained about being demi-sexual, he'd said he needed to feel a connection.

The elevator at the end of the hallway pinged and a small group of women spilled out, laughing and chatting as they walked in my direction.

I needed to make a decision. Walk past the women toward the elevators or return to the room and face my best friend. After what had happened over the last few days, I suddenly became paralyzed and unable to make a decision.

"Hey, you all right there?" one of the women asked. "You get locked out? That happened to us a few days ago. You'd think five bad-ass women would have it better together, right? Nope. A vacation from life apparently means a vacation from braining." The other women all laughed with her.

She looked nice in a yellow-and-pink striped summer dress, barely-there makeup, and sandals. Her eyes were warm and sympathetic as she waited for my reply. In another world, she would have been the kind of woman I'd go for, but right now, I couldn't think of anything I wanted less.

"Um, no, I'm not locked out."

Her brows met in the middle, and she looked at the other women before turning back to me. "Are you sure you're okay? I can call reception for help. I'm not a doctor, but you look a little shaken."

I smiled. "I'm okay. Honestly. You all go enjoy your evening."

She smiled back and joined the group as they continued down the hall.

Escaping was no longer an option. River was probably ready and waiting for me, so I had to dust myself off and go back into the room to get ready for dinner.

Hopefully, I was good enough of an actor that River wouldn't be able to tell I'd overheard such an intimate moment. Not only that, but I'd liked it, and given the choice, I would have wanted to watch and maybe even join in.

How fucked up was that?

13

———

RIVER

"I can't believe we're going home tomorrow," Emery said, piercing the succulent kālua pig with his fork and bringing it to his mouth.

"Yeah, we blinked, and it's over," Noah said, stretching out on a blanket beside Lior. "Australia was amazing, and I'm glad we did this too, but there's something about being in your own bed, you know?"

"Absolutely," Lex agreed, rolling his neck before taking the forkful of food Emery fed him.

Adam remained silent, lying back, arms behind his head, gazing at the sky.

I'd spent the week forcing myself to relax while hyper-aware of Adam's constant presence by my side. I'd known it would be like this. The couples gravitated to each other, so there was just us left.

We were best friends. We'd seen each other almost every day for years. But a week ago, I'd been ready to hand in my notice at the restaurant and leave. Take a break from the ache in my heart over someone I knew I'd never have.

Now, as the aroma of roasted meat and pineapple wafted

through the air, mingling with the salty tang of the ocean breeze, I didn't know anything anymore.

"I will certainly miss the Hawaiian food," I said as the haupia's coconut richness melted on my tongue.

Around us, laughter punctuated the rhythmic beat of the ukulele, which I'd learned on this vacation was an import from Portuguese immigrants when they emigrated to the island from Madeira in the 1800s.

As the sun dipped lower, casting long shadows on the beach, Noah burst into the crowd's center with the infectious energy of someone who refused to be anything but the life of the party. "Come on, baby. Let's dance." He grabbed Lior's wrist, yanking him from the edge of the blanket where he sat beside Lex and Emery.

Lex must have noticed the panic in Emery's eyes because he turned to his fiancé and said, "Are you ready for dessert? I saw some people with ice cream."

"Sold," Emery replied, standing like his feet were springs.

Adam laughed. With his hair tousled by the sea breeze and his blue eyes reflecting the twilight, he got up and joined his older brother. His movements were not the practiced steps of the hula dancers who had performed earlier. Adam's hips moved with a rhythm all their own.

I stayed put, praying he wouldn't come get me because this was one of those rare moments when I got to just stare at him and let my guard down. I loved him from afar, and without anyone's eyes on me, I didn't have to pretend. Just for a moment.

Watching him, I was acutely aware of the suitcase waiting in the hotel room. In the morning, everything would change again, and I still hadn't made a decision.

As the song neared its end and the tempo slowed, our eyes met across the distance. His smile reached me, warm and open, beckoning me closer—an invitation or maybe a challenge.

When I shook my head, his smile wavered a little, but it was soon back on his lips as he turned around to dance with Noah and Lior.

The luau ended, the fire dancers extinguishing their flames with flourishes that drew the final round of applause as everyone settled under the waning light of the last flickering tiki torches.

I'd expected Adam to sit beside me on my blanket, but he walked past me toward the shore.

I turned and watched him from where I sat, considering how he must be feeling.

With Noah back from his honeymoon, the three brothers would be back in the office, working together like they had since they'd founded Spencer Brothers PR Agency. But with Lex and Noah in domestic bliss, where did that leave Adam?

He'd been the first to get engaged. But since then, both his brothers had not only found their own partners, they'd found their soulmates. The kind of connection I only ever read about in the hundreds of romance novels on my bookshelves at home.

I stood to join Adam.

"Find any good stars?" I asked, hoping to coax him away from whatever worry was creasing his forehead.

"Trying to," he replied with a half-smile that didn't quite reach his eyes. "But I think they're all hiding tonight."

"Or maybe they're just waiting for the right moment to shine.".

"Maybe."

He shifted uneasily in the sand. Our conversation had lulled into a comfortable silence, but it was clear the quiet only masked the thoughts raging in his mind.

"Something on your mind?" I ventured.

He released a sigh. "It's just… Victoria might come back, you know? And even if she doesn't…" He paused, swallowing hard. "I can't crash with Lex or Noah. They have their own lives, and…I'm really happy they've got Emery and Lior. I really am…"

"But it's not easy being around two loved-up couples."

"Yeah."

The thought of Victoria returning to Adam's life, even briefly, bothered me. She didn't deserve a second of his time, but I knew he'd give it to her because that was the man he was.

He needed answers, and he deserved them. I couldn't give him those, but I could give him a sanctuary, a place to call home, even if temporarily.

"Hey, Adam," I began, the words forming with a nervous clarity. "You know you always have a place with me, right? If you're looking for somewhere to stay…"

His eyes met mine, wide with a mixture of surprise and contemplation. A moment lingered between us, charged with something I couldn't name, and for the first time since I'd met Adam, it wasn't my imagination conjuring something that wasn't there.

"Like college?" he asked, a hopeful note threading through his voice. "Aren't we too old for that?"

"I'm sure we can still do it without the questionable décor and Ramen diet," I assured him, a smile teasing the corners of my lips despite the flutter of nerves in my stomach.

"All right," Adam decided, his hesitation gone. "Let's do it."

We settled on the soft, moonlit sand, a world away from the laughter and chatter of the fading luau. I stretched out my legs, feeling grains cling to my skin.

"Remember how you used to decorate our college dorm

with those thrift shop finds?" he chuckled. "We had more wicker furniture than an outdoor patio sale."

I laughed. "Yeah, and let's not forget your impressive collection of band posters. The walls looked like a shrine to music festivals we never attended."

"Guilty," he confessed. "But hey, at least this time around, we'll have actual furniture. And no roommates who steal our food or use our toothpaste."

"True," I agreed, nudging him playfully with my shoulder. "And you know you'll never starve around me."

Adam's face softened, and he turned to me. "That sounds…really nice, River. Too bad you still can't convince me that kale chips are a substitute for real snacks."

"Give it time," I teased.

He met my gaze, and for a heartbeat, the playful banter gave way to something charged and unspoken.

As we stood to join the others, my heart raced with the possibility of what lay ahead. This time together would be different. We were grown up and had our own careers. And besides, this was only temporary. Soon, Adam would find a new place to live, and he'd move on again.

"Why are you grinning like someone who got a free dessert?" Lex asked Adam.

"Because I've got a temporary place to live." He ran his hands through his already messy hair. "I didn't realize how much it was stressing me out not having a place to go to and not knowing when or if Victoria will come back."

"Where are you going? You know you can stay with us, right? I mean, if you don't mind Gordon perving on you while you sleep, the guest room is yours."

"Thanks…I think?" Adam laughed. "As much as I love your voyeur gecko, I'm going to stay with River. Just like the old days, right?" He tapped my shoulder and then went off to the dessert table to get his hands on the last of the haupia.

"River…" Noah's voice broke through the quiet, his tone carrying a weight that immediately put me on edge. "Are you sure about this—living with Adam again?"

I glanced over at him and then at Lex, who wore the same expression. "Why wouldn't I be?"

Noah leaned closer. "Because," he began, his gaze steady on mine, "it's different now. You're different."

My heart thumped erratically against my ribcage, but I feigned ignorance. "I don't follow."

He exhaled slowly, searching my face for something I wasn't ready to reveal. "I've seen the way you look at him, River. There's more there than just friendship, isn't there?"

A lump formed in my throat, and I struggled to maintain my composure. The hidden truth of my feelings for Adam—feelings I had meticulously buried under layers of camaraderie and distance—threatened to spill over.

"Adam's my best friend," I said, my voice barely above a whisper.

Noah's eyes softened, but his next words held an edge of warning. "I want to say go for it and don't give up. Fuck knows it somehow worked for me, but Adam's straight…or at least he thinks he is. I don't want you to get hurt."

"Nothing's changed," I lied, my voice steadier than I felt. "We're just two friends helping each other out."

"Okay," Noah said, though I could tell he wasn't entirely convinced. He clapped a hand on my shoulder in a gesture that was both supportive and cautionary. "Just be careful, all right?"

I nodded, not trusting myself to speak further on the matter as Adam returned with a tray filled with haupia. "Boys, this is what happens when my flirting game is on point. Who's hungry for more dessert?"

14

———

ADAM

"Honey, I'm home!" I joked as I toed off my shoes. I rounded the hallway into the living room, finding River in his favorite place: sitting in the wide armchair with a book in his hands, wearing his favorite book-quotes pajama pants and an old college T-shirt.

"Welcome back, dear," River chuckled without moving his gaze away from the book.

"Are the kids in bed?" I sat on the couch, placing my socked feet on the coffee table.

"Artemis was an angel, but Augustus put up a fight."

I bit my lips closed so I wouldn't laugh as River looked up from the book that had two semi-naked men embracing on the cover. "You picked the names. You should know they come with an attitude."

"It's your turn to put them to bed tomorrow. You know how I feel about consistency. Don't ruin my hard work, dear."

And then he went back to the book, his shoulders shaking as he tried to contain his own laugh.

"Hmm. You know what this means." I leaned over and whispered, "We can make sweet love all night long."

I stood and went over to my room to get ready for a shower as River let out a belly laugh.

The joke had started when I'd come home from work on River's first day off since I'd moved in and had startled him with my arrival. Usually, I was in bed by the time he got in from the restaurant. Some days, he was up before me to go to the fish market, and some days, I left before he was up.

The whole thing had escalated to me finding River one evening in the kitchen, barefoot, in his book-quotes pajama pants and apron—no shirt—cooking dinner, and now it seemed we already had fictitious children.

I wrapped a towel around my waist and stepped into our shared bathroom. My cock hardened as the scent of River's body wash filled my nostrils. I was like Pavlov's dog. One whiff of the smell and I was back in the hotel room, listening to the sounds of him jerking off. My name on his lips as he came. And what it all meant.

Like every other day since I'd moved in with River, I ignored the need to touch myself. At first, I'd tried to think of anything other than River, but my dick wasn't cooperating. As soon as I'd picture the curves of some imaginary woman, sucking her nipples into sweet peaks or kissing her soft skin, my erection deflated faster than a balloon with a pinprick hole.

I was going out of my mind and didn't know what to do. The obvious was too risky. How could I tell River I spent my awake moments thinking about his body against mine and how, instead of grossing me out, it lit a fire within me? How could I tell him that suddenly, his lips were the most fascinating thing in the world? How could I tell him I didn't know what it all meant and was scared to do something wrong and lose him.

I'd read more about demisexuality, and with every passing day since that last night at the hotel, I wondered more and more if River felt something more than just friendship for me. But his behavior hadn't changed. He treated me just like he always had. A best friend.

A rough laugh escaped me as I stepped into the warm shower. I was still hurting from what Victoria did, but the thought of losing River like I did Victoria? That was so unfathomable that I'd decided there was no way I could ever risk it.

So, in two short weeks, I'd resigned myself to living with blue balls until this phase passed. It would, right?

When I returned to the living room, the smell of tomato sauce pulled me toward the kitchen.

"If my parents ever find out your favorite food is Italian, you'll be so fired," I joked.

"You will keep your mouth shut, Adam Spencer."

I joined him by the stove, where he was stirring the sauce with one hand and the pasta with the other.

"Or what?" I teased.

"Or your enjoyment of this food will be relegated to smelling it from afar."

"Now that's just mean."

He glanced at me, a smile teasing his lips. Those fucking full lips.

I cleared my throat, looking away. "Need a hand?"

"Sure," he said, oblivious to the errant thoughts inside my head. "Can you grab the Parmesan?"

I moved closer, our bodies almost touching as I looked for the cheese I assumed was already on the counter. My breath hitched at the proximity. River's gaze met mine, and he smiled. "Fridge."

"Yes. I knew that." I turned my back to him to open the

fridge. The cool air brushed against my skin, but it did nothing to stop the heat that flushed my skin.

He drained the pasta and turned the heat off the sauce. His practiced moves as he grated the cheese over the sauce were mesmerizing, and I had to force myself to look away.

"I'll set the table," I said, grabbing two glasses from the cupboard.

We moved around each other comfortably, grabbing utensils and drinks until we sat at his table facing each other. I didn't miss how domestic it all felt.

My throat tightened for a second. I'd had this domesticity with Victoria, at least when we first moved in together. Then, she was always away on business trips or working late, and usually, I'd end up having dinner alone.

"What's that face for?" River asked.

"Sorry. I was just thinking."

"About what?"

"Victoria." I sighed. "It's been a long time since I've been in the kitchen while someone else is making dinner, and then we eat together."

River furrowed his brows. "I'm sorry. I didn't know."

"Of course you didn't. I guess…maybe I've unknowingly been pretending everything was okay with Victoria and me. So much that I hadn't realized we really weren't okay. Maybe her leaving was the best thing. She was braver than me. I would have married her, and one day, I would have opened my eyes and realized we weren't truly together anymore."

River put his fork on his plate with a clink. "Nothing will convince me she didn't do this for herself. She wasn't thinking of you, Adam. If she were, she would have called it off before you had a hundred guests paying to stay at an expensive vineyard hotel. Not to mention the rest of the bill. Speaking of which, have you spoken to your parents?"

I cringed. "No. I've been avoiding them actually."

"I know."

Of course he did. Even though my parents were meant to be semi-retired now that River was running the restaurant, they couldn't stay away.

"Let me guess, they've been low-case grilling you at work."

He snorted. "No low-case about that. Your parents have practically sat me down and interrogated me about how you've been."

"I'm sorry."

"They're worried." His voice carried a distinct layer of protectiveness.

"I know. It's just…hard to talk to them. I feel like such a failure."

River reached over the table and grabbed my hand. "This is not on you. Whatever issues you and Victoria might have been having, whether you were aware of them or not, are not an excuse for her to do what she did."

"Yeah, I know."

"Do you?"

I sat up straight and took my hand back, holding the glass of water. "What do you mean?"

"I mean that you still haven't gone back to your apartment to grab your stuff, and as much as I don't mind you raiding my closet, I think that's something you need to do."

The pasta suddenly tasted like cardboard, so I took a gulp of water.

"I'll do it this week."

He sighed. "I'm not trying to pressure you, but…"

"But what?"

"Never mind." He stood to wash his plate and cup.

I hadn't finished my dinner, but I'd lost my appetite. When I took my plate to the sink, River turned to me, and before I knew it, I was on the receiving end of a River hug.

My throat tightened. I hadn't had a real River hug in so long that I hadn't known I'd missed it. I wrapped my arms around him and allowed myself the closeness.

When I pulled back, a small tear fell down my cheek.

"I really wish things were different," he said, gently wiping away the tear with his thumb, a sad smile gracing his lips.

"Me too." Although we were probably wishing for different things. I knew River hated seeing me hurt, so it didn't bother me much that he was more vocal now about his dislike for Victoria. He wasn't wrong about the things she'd done.

We stood there for the longest time. Too close for friends but at the same time not close enough. My pulse picked up with every breath he took as I wondered how long it would take until I felt somewhat like my old self again.

THE CLINK of silverware and the hum of conversation at Lusitana were usually comforting, but today, each sound grated on me.

"Hey, Earth to River." Drew's voice cut through my thoughts. He leaned against the bar, towel slung over his shoulder, eyebrows knotted while studying me. "You're looking more stormy than usual. Something up?"

I met Drew through Noah months ago when we discovered Noah was volunteering at the Foundation Drew and his foster brother West had founded to support young people and children in foster care and from disadvantaged backgrounds.

The success and support the foundation had received from the community came down to Drew and West's hard work. All while maintaining jobs to support themselves.

Every cent they raised went straight back to the charity and the kids.

When West was laid off a couple months ago, I gave him a job as a bartender at the restaurant.

The staff loved him, and so did the customers. It didn't

hurt that he was a damned good bartender, even if sometimes all too perceptive.

I forced my eyes away from the spot where Adam had sat hours earlier with his parents, the hollow feeling in my chest expanding. "It's nothing," I lied.

"Come on, man, you can talk to me. Guy problems?"

I hesitated, then sighed, my defenses crumbling like the crust of the lemon tarts on our dessert menu. "I just… I don't know how to deal with all this space he's taking up—not just here, but here." I tapped a finger against my temple, then against the left side of my chest.

Drew's hand lingered on my shoulder. "Have you considered just talking to the guy about this? About how you're feeling?"

"Talk to him?" My voice was a strangled whisper. "And say what, Drew? 'Hey, by the way, your existence is throwing my entire world off balance?'"

Drew's eyes softened with empathy. "Trust me when I say I know exactly how you feel, and I'm totally asking you to do as I say and not as I do because fuck knows I'm never going to do anything about it. But what's stopping *you?*"

I turned to him, measuring my words carefully so I wouldn't give too much away. "You're in love with West, aren't you?"

His eyes widened. "I'm going to murder Noah."

I chuckled. "Why?"

"Because he opened his mouth. That's why."

"Don't go on a killing spree just yet." I leaned closer to the bar. "I just saw the way you looked at West when we were helping you at the old hospital months ago. I'm sure he's unaware of it."

"Then you know why I can't do what I'm telling you to do. If I tell West I have feelings for him, he's going to be all grossed out, and I'll lose him."

"Why?"

He huffed, picking up a glass and cleaning it. "Because we're brothers, and apparently, that's frowned upon."

"Dude, you're foster brothers. You grew up in the same place, not out of the same vagina."

"Ew. Please don't say that again."

"True though. So, what's the real excuse?"

He shrugged. "Isn't it obvious? I don't want to lose him. If he doesn't feel the same way, it'll be awkward. We've always had each other's backs. We built the Star Finders Foundation from nothing. I can't give all that up. It's too great a risk."

"And you don't think the potential gain would be worth it?"

He smiled wistfully. "When I think of the gain? Yes. To finally be with"—he shook his head like he was trying to shake the whole thought off— "but he hasn't given me any hints that what he feels for me is anything but brotherly love. The kind of bond that comes from growing up in the system together."

He put the glass down and stared at me.

"You're really good at deflecting, Mister Boss. I got tricked for a moment there, but you're not getting out of it that easy. Why can't you tell this guy how you feel?"

Dammit.

"Because it's complicated. Like, foster brothers complicated, except we're not foster brothers."

"I'm lost. Who's this guy? Do I know him?"

My fingers tightened around the polished countertop of the bar, the cool surface grounding me as I grappled with the notion of laying bare the feelings I'd kept hidden for so long.

"It's Adam."

Drew gasped. "Adam as in…*Adam*, Adam?"

"How many Adams do you know?"

"Fuck, dude. Yeah, I get it. You're best friends, and you don't want to mess with that."

I nodded. "Not to mention he's straight."

"You sure about that?"

No. I wasn't sure about that. Not anymore. The lingering looks. The way he touched me like he wanted to do more of it but didn't know how. The way his eyes settled on my mouth every time we were alone together? No. I wasn't sure he was straight. But coming to terms with your sexuality wasn't easy, and while Adam had grown up with two queer brothers, thinking you're straight all your life and then finding you might not be, has to screw with your head.

If. *If* what I was reading into his behavior was correct.

"Your silence is loud and clear," Drew said.

One of the servers came over to the bar to place an order so I took my position by the front desk and checked if we still had any bookings tonight.

I was helping out by placing the chairs on the tables after we closed when Drew appeared beside me.

"I've been thinking about it."

"About what?"

"I think you should start paying attention to Adam and then make a move."

I laughed. "Pot meet kettle."

"Well, I'm a hopeless case, but—"

"And I'm not? At least West is gay. What hope do I have?"

"Okay. Here's an idea. When you tell Adam, I'll tell West."

I almost dropped the chair on my feet. "You're joking."

"Nope. Dead serious."

I laughed. "Well, I guess we're both going to be pining for the foreseeable future."

He shrugged and left me to my chair-stacking.

I wiped down the last table, the cloth gliding over the surface in slow circles before I stacked the last four chairs, ready for the cleaner in the morning.

The conversation with Drew was stuck on repeat in my head.

All the what-ifs flew around my mind, giving me glimpses of hope but also moments of desperation. Imagining Adam's reaction to finding out his best friend wasn't the person he thought.

Would he feel betrayed that I'd kept this secret from him? Because I'd basically been living my life pretending to be just Adam's best friend. He'd accepted my friendship with the knowledge that that's all it was.

As I got into my car to drive home, I was still unclear about what to do, but one thing was certain, I didn't have to do anything.

In a few more weeks, Adam would start looking for a place to live, and when he was no longer filling my space with all the amazing things that were Adam, I'd start to move on. Maybe I'd even pick up my travel plans.

The light in the living room was on when I pulled into the driveway. Adam was usually asleep when I came home from working the closing shift at the restaurant, so I was immediately worried.

I rushed inside to find Adam surrounded by boxes, sitting on the floor with a stack of photos in his hand.

"No one prints photos anymore," he said, his voice devoid of emotion. "I did it in the beginning because I wanted to have a memory photo album like my grandmother and parents have. I always asked about the people who had been important enough in my family's life that they got their picture taken. Not only that, they made it into an actual album. It's interesting, right?"

I removed my shoes and dropped my jacket and keys on the couch before sitting next to him.

"What happened?"

"After lunch with my parents, I decided to go back to Victoria's apartment for my stuff. I'd never realized until then how little I had there."

He looked at me, confusion and hurt all over his face.

"I had a whole apartment filled with things that were mine before I moved in with her, but somehow, without me noticing, those things made their way to goodwill, or they were sold. This is my whole life, River." He pointed at the boxes. "I'm thirty years old, and my life fits in a few boxes."

I took the photos from his hand, put them on the coffee table, and then held both his hands in mine. "These are just material things, Adam. *You,* the essence of Adam Spencer, is the memories you make or the way in which you were dealt a shitty hand and turned it into a Vegas jackpot."

He shook his head like he didn't believe what I was saying.

"You are more than this, okay? You will rebuild your life just the way you want it, and this time, you're not going to settle for anything less than being swept off your feet by someone who can love you the same way you're capable of loving others. With that person, you're going to pick what you take into the next stage of your life and what you let go of."

He squeezed my hands back and nodded.

"Come here." I pulled him onto my lap, which wasn't easy since we were practically the same size. I opened the drawer in the coffee table and pulled out my old iPod—remembering how I'd teased Adam in Hawaii for still using his when I'd known where mine was and still used it occasionally. I pressed the button and thanked old technology for longer-lasting battery life.

I put one of the earbuds in Adam's ear and the other in mine and pressed play. I didn't have to pick a song. They were all good. The songs we'd picked together over the years.

My own feelings were set aside to return to a place I hadn't been for so long that I'd almost forgotten it once existed.

River and Adam's Awesome Playlist.

I stayed still until the battery gave up the ghost.

"Thank you, River," Adam said, leaning against the door to his room after we'd left everything behind in the living room.

"Any time."

He turned around to go inside. "Love you."

My breath caught for a split second before I managed, "Love you back."

16

———

ADAM

I HESITATED, my hand hovering over River's bedroom door.

After my breakdown last night, I'd slept like a baby. When my alarm clock went off this morning, I couldn't move.

Going to work and pretending I wasn't going through a huge life crisis was more than I could handle today. So, I messaged my brothers and told them I needed the day.

They agreed without question, which meant our mom had likely told them I'd gone to Victoria's place to get my stuff yesterday and they knew I needed the space to process.

If only they knew how much I needed to process.

But after staring at the ceiling of River's spare room for ten minutes, I had an idea. A quick call to West and I had more than a plan.

I opened River's door and flung myself at him.

"Fucking fuck," he cried under my weight. "You used to be lighter."

"I used to be a lot of things." I dug my fingers into his ribs, which was a ticklish area for him. He squirmed under me, which was when I felt his morning wood. Of course my confused and deranged dick had to react.

Fuck. Bad idea.

I moved quickly off him and stole his pillow, covering his head with it.

"You can't just walk into people's rooms like this. What if I was jerking off?" His voice was muffled under the pillow.

"You weren't because I didn't hear you moan my name."

"Asshole."

He managed to grab the pillow and push it off him. It ended up between us, so I pulled it over my lap, hoping by the time I told him about my plan, I wouldn't have an awkward walk out of the room.

"Hey, let's play hooky today. Just you and me," I said.

"It's my day off," he chuckled.

"Fine. I'll play hooky then."

"What do you have in mind?"

"Get dressed, and you'll soon find out."

I flung the pillow back at him and ran out of his bedroom.

By the time River came out, dressed and ready to go, I had myself and my dick under control.

The bell above the door to Margot's Ice Cream Parlor jingled as we stepped inside, the familiar scents of vanilla, sugar, and coffee wrapping around us.

When Margot opened, she hired our agency to help her with the launch. The campaign went viral, and Margot became a staple in Cliffborough.

Initially, she only offered her homemade ice cream but had since started opening earlier and offering breakfast. Emery was completely obsessed, as seen in his social media feed, which was practically an homage to Margot's ice cream, Lex, and their pets Gordon the gecko and Goldie the fish.

"Taking the day off, huh?" River teased as we picked a table by the window. His light-green eyes seemed brighter in the morning sunshine, almost aquamarine. How had I never noticed that? "What's the occasion?"

"Missed this," I admitted as I picked up the menu, gesturing between us.

The server appeared, her cheery demeanor adding to the morning's charm.

"Good morning, gentlemen. What can I get for you today?" she asked.

"Can I have Margot's special stack?" I asked.

"Bacon and ice cream?"

"Absolutely."

She smiled. "How about you, sir?" she asked River.

He shook his head, a smile curling up his lips. "Hell, why not? I'll have the same."

"Six months working here and it's still my favorite," she said. "Would you like coffee?"

"Yes, please," we said at the same time.

When she left, River leaned forward on the table.

"So, are you going to let me in on this crazy plan you have?"

I snorted. "I didn't say it was crazy."

"You woke me up by jumping on me."

"That's fair. I don't want to reveal too much. Just go with the flow."

He raised a brow.

"You're becoming pretty good at that," he said.

"At what?"

"Going with the flow. Being knocked down and then standing and dusting yourself off like nothing happened."

I looked at the world outside the window. A few people

ran on the pavement by the river. There were a few mothers with strollers and old ladies walking arm in arm as they talked.

"What's the point in staying down? Taking you and my brothers on my pseudo-honeymoon was the best decision I could have made at the time. If I stay home feeling sorry for myself, what am I telling the universe? That I'm just the stuff in those boxes? Nah. It's time to find out who Adam Spencer is."

As I said that, the server came with our order. Pancakes piled high, strips of crispy bacon peeking out from under a generous scoop of ice cream, and plenty of coffee to wash it all down.

"And right now, I'm going to be the Adam who can eat a breakfast bigger than my head, just like we used to do when we were cramming for finals and having one good meal a day."

River held up his fist, so I bumped it. We didn't need any more words.

We fell into a rhythm of conversation as we polished off our breakfast fueled by the best coffee. We talked about everything and nothing, just like the old times.

"Feels like it's been ages since we've done this," River said.

"Too long," I agreed. "And it's mostly my fault. I know I wasn't as available when I was with Victoria. To be honest, it all seems like a different lifetime, like I was a different person."

"You don't have to apologize. When you're in a relationship, the other person takes priority. It's normal to want to stay in or go out with them."

I cut a chunk of syrupy pancake with my fork and brought it to my mouth, moaning over the perfect flavor and texture.

When I looked up, River's gaze was on my mouth. When his eyes met mine, I looked away quickly.

"It's not that I didn't want to go out with you or my brothers," I continued. "It sounds like such a ridiculous excuse now, but Victoria wanted us to hang out together at home, and she traveled so much as it was that I also craved those moments with her."

"Like I said—"

"I also craved moments with you, but I didn't know how to make it happen without Victoria going off the rails," I interrupted because I needed him to know it. "I still don't understand why she disliked you. Did something happen between you two?"

"Sort of. After you guys became serious, there was one time we went out to Tanner's and got drunk. You crashed at my place afterward. The next time I met her, she made it clear she thought I was a bad influence."

"I didn't know that. I'm so sorry, River."

He shrugged. "In a perfect world, our best friends will find a partner we can be friends with too. The world isn't perfect."

The clink of cutlery against our empty plates marked the end of breakfast. I wiped my mouth with a napkin as I caught River's gaze.

"Let's take a walk by the river," he suggested.

"It's like you know my master plan for today. Let's grab the check."

We crossed the road to the Riverwalk, walking side by side.

I reached into my pocket, pulling out my old iPod, scratched and worn from years of use. I offered one earbud to River.

As the first notes of one of our songs passed my eardrums, I closed my eyes for a second and breathed in the morning air. I let the music transport me back to those care-free college days when the future was a distant concern and our only worry was scoring the next hookup and passing exams.

When the first chords of the next song played, we both stopped and looked at each other, grinning. Europe's "The Final Countdown" had been the song that always brought a smile to our faces. The infectious cadence had brought us out of many funks. We couldn't not sing along.

People walking past stared at us with a smile. Even our out-of-tune performance was enough to make the world a better place. When the song ended, we were doubled over laughing, our voices hoarse from the strain.

"Fuck, I needed that," River said.

"Yeah, that was fun. Are you ready for the next stage of our hooky day?" I asked.

"Again. I'm not playing hooky. You are."

"Details." I shrugged.

We crossed the bridge and headed back toward the car.

"Are you going to tell me where we're going?" he asked.

"We're going to the Star Finders Foundation."

River stopped abruptly.

"Why?"

"They need help."

"They always need help. Why today?"

What was going on? River was always ready to spend time at the foundation helping out. Why was he being weird today?

"Well, we have time today. Unless you have other plans. I mean, you didn't mention anything."

"No…I don't have plans. It's just…never mind. Let's go."

He resumed walking, so I had to take a couple of quick steps to catch up.

"What's up? I can call West and cancel if you want."

"West?"

"Yeah, he's there all day today. Drew is working, which you should know because he works for you."

"Oh. Um…okay. Sorry, that was probably a little weird."

I chuckled. "If you agree you're playing hooky with me today, I'll let it slide."

River laughed and put his arm over my shoulder. "Fine. I'm playing hooky. Even though it's my day off," he muttered under his breath.

"Come on. We don't want to be late."

The old hospital building was on the edge of the city, which was convenient because it was closer to where so many of the kids Drew and West wanted to help lived.

Several cars and bikes were in the parking lot, and the door to the old emergency room waiting area was open.

West was behind the glass, surrounded by paperwork.

"Is this where we come for emergencies?" I joked.

West raised his head and smiled. "Fuck no. But if you want to break your back painting a few rooms and get paid in bad coffee, you're in the right place."

"I guess we're in the right place," I said.

"Painting rooms?" River whispered next to me.

"Yup."

West handed us a couple of paint coveralls and pointed to the first room in the hallway. A couple of cans of paint and rollers were in the middle of the room. All the furniture had been removed and West had told me the floors would all be stripped and redone so we didn't have to worry about making a mess.

"Ready to make this place even brighter?" I asked, handing River a roller.

"How about a little competition?" he asked, dipping it into the tray of sky-blue paint.

"You're on. I take these two walls, and you take those two? We meet in the middle."

We high-fived and got to it.

Working side by side, our movements fell into a familiar rhythm, the swish of brushes and rollers the only noise in the room, other than the voices in the distance from other volunteers working in different areas of the building. Occasionally, I caught River's eye, and something unspoken passed between us.

"Look at you two, synchronized painters," West remarked with a chuckle, breaking our trance as he stuck his head through the door. "Could've made a career out of this."

"Missed our calling," I quipped back.

"Keep up the good work. There's a few more rooms, and I intend on milking every second of your time here."

River laughed. "You got it, boss."

By the time we stepped back to admire our work, the room was filled with light and color.

"Looks great, doesn't it?" River asked.

"More than great,"

"Thanks for today, Adam."

"Anytime." I couldn't help but tease River about the streak of paint on his cheek. "You're supposed to be painting walls, River, not your face."

He chuckled, wiping at his cheek with the back of his hand, only managing to smear the paint further. "It's a new fashion statement," he said, flashing a grin that crinkled the corners of his eyes.

"Remember when you tried to dye your hair blue to impress Jake What's-His-Name?" I asked.

"Let's not," he said with a playful grimace. "I ended up looking like a Smurf for weeks."

"Hey, he did say it was unforgettable," I pointed out,

remembering how we'd laughed until our sides hurt when River showed up at my house, his hair a vibrant disaster.

"Unforgettable is one word for it."

I paused, brush in mid-air, as a particular memory surfaced. "Do you remember the pact we made? That no matter where we ended up, we'd always find our way back to each other?"

"Of course," River said. "Like gravity. No matter what happened, we'd gravitate back."

"Seems like gravity's done its job." My voice was barely a whisper as I realized we had drifted closer.

I swallowed dry as my eyes gravitated toward River's lips. When my gaze met his, I saw it because I recognized it. Attraction. Want.

I'm demisexual. I remembered the exact words he'd spoken that evening on the beach. *I can't feel attraction to someone unless there's an emotional bond first. A real connection.*

Today had been a day for us to reconnect as friends and build on the time we'd spent together in Hawaii, but it had also driven us closer. If I'd had any doubt River could feel attraction for me, his eyes were loud and clear.

His lips were parted, and when his tongue wet his lips, I released a quiet moan.

"River," I whispered.

"Hey, guys," West said before entering the room. We jumped back like we'd been electrocuted. I didn't dare make eye contact with River. "Well done here. This looks great. If you're up for doing another room, that would be great."

"Yeah, sure," River said, picking up the bucket with paint and the brushes and leaving the room.

ADAM WAS RIGHT. I was playing hooky, but it was from my life, from making good decisions, from treating my best friend like a best friend.

Fuck.

I'd almost kissed Adam. If West hadn't come in, I would have done it. He'd been so close I could smell his body wash, *my body wash*. His blue eyes had gone darker, and the way they were fixed on my mouth? My brain got ideas. It got stupid ideas that maybe Adam wanted to kiss me as much as I wanted to kiss him.

What a fucking stupid idea, right?

I placed the can of paint on the floor of the next room and uncovered the one that was already there.

"It's pink," Adam said.

I turned around. He looked like nothing had just happened.

"Yeah. I'll put this one outside and clean the rollers so they don't get mixed up," I said, taking everything outside while Adam got started on the painting.

The rest of the afternoon went by in a flash. We ended up

taking on a third bedroom, so by the time we finished, West was delighted with the progress, treating us to tacos he got delivered to the center.

"For real, guys," he said. "You've shaved a couple of days off our list. These tacos are delicious but in no way repay what you've done."

Adam chuckled. "That's why we call it volunteering. We're happy to be able to help, right, River?"

I nodded. "I'd be happy to come back on my next day off."

West rested his elbows on his knees, wringing a napkin between his fingers. Suddenly, he looked really tired.

"Thank you, River. We really appreciate it. You know, with both Drew and I working full-time, we're reliant on support from volunteers. The hospital building is perfect, but it's fucking huge, and even with our plan to work on it in stages, it's still a lot."

"Could you hire people in addition to the volunteers?" Adam asked.

"Not enough money to really make a difference."

"We should plan a fundraiser. Do you mind if I workshop something with my brothers?"

West smiled. "Not at all."

We helped West clear up all the trash and then left.

The closest we got to my place, the more anxious I became. I couldn't stop replaying that moment in the blue room. Was it a one-off? Would it happen again? And if it did, would it end with us kissing? And then what?

I didn't notice we were actually inside the house with our shoes and coats off until Adam turned to me and cleared his throat.

"Have you—" he hesitated like he was weighing his question. "Have you ever tried…hooking up? Was it different for you?"

"I did. College life, remember?" He shrugged. "But it felt hollow. Experimenting taught me something crucial—I crave depth. A connection that isn't just about how someone looks, but about how he makes me feel."

"Is that what you're looking for now?" His gaze pierced through the defenses I'd been building since the moment in the blue room.

"Isn't that what we all want?" I asked, my heart drumming against my ribs. "To be seen and understood beyond the superficial?"

He nodded. "Yeah," he whispered, almost to himself. "Beyond the superficial."

My heart clenched at those words, at the raw honesty in his tone, like he truly got it. Was he just reaffirming our friendship, or was there something else, something deeper, simmering beneath the surface?

"River," he said cautiously, "when we talk about connections, about depth…do you ever think that maybe—"

"Maybe what?" I turned to face him fully, his eyes searching, questioning, almost imploring.

"*We* have that connection, right?" His hand reached out, hovering in the air before resting nervously on my chest. The touch was electric, even through the layers of fabric.

"Of course. You're my best friend," I reassured him. Or maybe I was reassuring myself. A reminder that's all we were, even if right now, with Adam so close again, I was on the brink of testing my resolve.

"What if…?" he whispered.

My heart hammered against my ribcage, ready to burst out. I swallowed the lump forming in my throat, acutely aware of how this conversation could shift the very foundation of our friendship.

"It's just that…" Adam's voice faltered, and he took a

deep breath. "Lately, I've been feeling something… Something new. Different."

CODE RED. CODE RED.

"New and different how?" I prompted, stepping closer.

"As in, I've never felt this way about anyone before. Not like this."

His confession hung in the air as I stood motionless, my entire being focused on the man before me. The fear and longing playing in his eyes that all of a sudden wasn't just my best friend Adam. He was the man I admired for his resilience, empathy, work ethic, kindness.

"Adam…" I started, trying to keep my voice as steady as I could. "I need you to remember that I'm gay, and you're… you're too close. You're confusing me."

A small smile curled his lips, and he licked them before dragging his teeth along his bottom lip.

"You know exactly what you're doing, don't you?" I asked.

"I don't. I'm so out of my league here, but…I want to try."

He leaned forward until his nose touched mine. My breath caught in my throat. I was too afraid to make a sudden move so I closed my eyes, waiting for the inevitable.

Please…

"May I kiss you, River?"

His barely-there voice was all the consent I needed.

I closed the little space between us and pressed my lips against his. It was a tentative brush at first. Questioning. Giving him the option to pull back.

When he didn't, my heart clenched, and I allowed myself to lean into the kiss, deepening it and leaving no room for doubt.

Adam's lips were as soft as I'd remembered, but even in my wildest fantasies, I never thought it could be like this. He pressed me against the wall, taking over. His hands wrapped around my neck, keeping me steadily in place as he took everything he wanted.

The unmistakable feel of a hard cock against mine had my eyes rolling to the back of my head. My brain became mush as I let him guide the kiss, taste me, ravish me.

I knew that once in his life, and now at least twice, it was clear Adam had no issues kissing a guy, but I was still too afraid to flip things over in case he realized what he was doing and stopped. Because I wanted remember this kiss for the rest of my life for all the good reasons. I was selfish like that.

His moans became louder. He rubbed against me, seeking relief.

Fuck, it felt so good.

I ran my hands over his shoulders, feeling the familiar contours beneath my palms, yet everything about this touch was different—it was charged. It was as if every moment we'd spent together recently, every laugh and lingering glance, had led us to this moment.

"River," Adam whispered against my lips, and fuck, I could come from the sound alone.

"You taste so fucking good, Adam," I whispered back.

Our kiss slowed, not ending but changing, becoming tender and affirming. With each peck, with my lips trapped between Adam's, I lost a little more of myself, and, in that moment, I didn't give two shits about it.

When we finally parted, we were both panting like we'd had a full round of sex. Our eyes met, and I held my breath, waiting for the moment he realized what he'd done.

All I saw was a smile.

"Wow. That was—"

"Unforgettable," I said, finishing his thought.

"Yeah."

We were the same height, so it would've been easy to reach out and kiss him again. I didn't allow myself the transgression. Not yet, at least.

When he pushed his lips forward to kiss me, I placed my hand between our mouths.

"If we keep doing this, I'm going to want more. Hell, I already do," I confessed. "But I think we should talk first."

He let out a breath. "Yeah, you're right. We should talk."

18

———

ADAM

My pulse hammered in my ears as I followed River to the living room, my lips tingling, my dick way too hard, and my brain too blood-deprived to hold a coherent thought.

River had questions. I got it. But how was I supposed to give him answers when I didn't have any? All I knew was that kissing River had shifted my alignment, and I was struggling to figure out which way was up.

A problem my dick clearly didn't have.

We sat facing each other on the bigger couch, and I couldn't help smiling at the situation.

"What's the grin for?" he asked, his smile mirroring mine.

"I kissed a boy and I liked it," I sang.

A cushion hit my face, and I laughed harder. Whatever had just happened, I was on a high. I could only imagine this was how it must feel to skydive, or go white-water rafting.

The kiss had been a revelation. River's lips had been firm, insistent, but also pliant. He'd let me take charge and given me time to adjust, but when he finally responded and took over, it had hit me like no other kiss in my whole life.

129

He'd left me dizzy and craving more. How could I get this conversation out of the way so we could get back to breathing each other's air?

"God, Adam, I have so many questions."

"Can we not bypass all that and go back to kissing? I'm so fucking hard."

He groaned and ran his hands over his face, scratching his short scruff.

"You're killing me here."

I shifted closer to him on the couch and put one arm over the back, holding my head in my hand. The other free hand pulled the string on his hoodie.

My mind raced with questions, doubts tangling with desire as I came to the realization that I wanted River in ways I couldn't fully comprehend.

"I wish I knew what to say, but this is as new to me as it is to you."

"You know, this isn't the first time we kissed."

It was my turn for my jaw to hit the ground.

River chuckled, and I looked at him. "Should I be hurt you don't remember?" he asked, and I couldn't tell if his smile was covering up hurt feelings.

I shook my head. "No, I remember it. I guess I haven't thought about it in a long time."

"You wanted to kiss the girl from English class you were dating, and you didn't want to mess it up, so you asked me to kiss you for practice."

I'd asked him for help with the kiss. My embarrassment was only slightly less than the mortification of kissing a girl and being bad at it. My dumb fourteen-year-old self hadn't enjoyed the kiss because I'd been too preoccupied with the technicalities.

As it was, while no catastrophes happened when I kissed

the girl, I'd also been disappointed at the nonevent. I couldn't even remember the girl's name now.

River put his hand on my chin and tilted my head so our eyes met.

"Is this some kind of experiment? Something to get back at Victoria with? Fuck, I hate that my head is going there, but, Adam, I've been your best friend since we were kids. You've never indicated that you have any interest in guys—until now."

I lowered my gaze to his hoodie, tracing the pattern of our college logo with my eyes.

"Honestly? I don't know when it started. Maybe it was a combination of lots of little moments between us. Maybe I'm traumatized from being jilted on my wedding day." I let out a choked laugh, and River held my hand. "I just know that for a few weeks, all I can think about is you. At first, I thought it was because I was relieved that we could finally spend time together without me having to justify it to Victoria or be sneaky about it, but…"

Fear stopped me. Fear of losing River or, worse, hurting him with my uncertainty. Could I even call it a bi-awakening when it was only River who stirred these feelings in me? Was it fair to explore this part of myself at the risk of his heart and our friendship?

"Figuring out your sexuality takes time," he said. "Even when you feel strongly about someone, it's okay to step back to ensure those feelings come from the right place."

"I don't want to hurt you. I just…can't stop thinking about you. I must have been really blind before to not notice the curve of your ass or the way you bite your plump lip when you're trying to figure something out or how strong and put-together you always look."

"Adam," he said, exasperation tinged with lust.

I drew in a shuddering breath. The intensity of our kiss

lingered on my lips like a phantom sensation. I needed more of it even as my rational side begged for caution.

"River, I—" My voice cracked.

"Shh." River's fingertips brushed my cheek. "We don't have to figure this out right now."

Except I felt the weight of urgency, the need to protect what we had even as I stood on the precipice of wanting more.

My hand trembled in his. "I—God, I'm sorry, River," I stammered.

"Sorry for what?" River asked, his voice barely above a whisper. We were seated on the edge of the couch, our knees touching and our hands still linked.

"Do you regret it?" he asked, and I didn't miss the vulnerability in his voice.

I placed my hands on either side of his face. "No," I breathed out without hesitation. "I don't. Since that night at Haven—dancing, laughing, the way the lights made your eyes shine… I was blind to it at the time, but now I can tell that's when it started. I haven't been able to shake you from my thoughts, River."

"But you were going to marry Victoria? What if she hadn't left?"

"I don't know. That morning, before you came into my room, I planned to marry her. Would these feelings have surfaced in the future and put my marriage on the line? I don't know. There's not much point in focusing on the what-ifs now."

"It's a lot to process."

"I know."

"Let's just take it one day at a time," he said.

"Okay." My hand trembled slightly, and River ran his thumb in circles over my skin, the touch sending an electric jolt through me.

We stood in silence for a moment, a contrast to all the loud thoughts in my head.

"Can I confess something?" I asked.

"I'm scared to say yes."

"I've thought about you," I said, "in ways I probably shouldn't have for a best friend…even touched myself, thinking of you." I dropped my gaze, a flush of heat creeping up my neck. Why was I telling him this? It could only push him away. "I'm…I just want you to know this has been building. It's not something I woke up today thinking about. It's been under my skin, itching to come out. You have to have noticed. I thought…"

I thought I'd noticed it in the way he looked at me. Was I wrong?

"Adam," River managed to choke out. "Maybe we should get some sleep."

"Talk about this another day?"

"Yeah, okay."

We walked through the hallway, stopping by the space between our rooms.

There was something else on my mind that I couldn't shake. "Can I ask you a question?"

"Of course."

"You got hard when we kissed."

"Adam," he groaned.

"No, I'm not trying to, you know… Well, I'm not gonna lie. I'd love a goodnight kiss and maybe a hand job." Hell, you don't ask, you don't get, right?

River pressed me against the wall, one hand placed by my head and the other on my waist.

"You're making it really difficult for me to do the right thing and leave you alone in your room."

I don't want you to leave me alone in my room.

I smiled. "That's the thing. I want to understand how this all fits with your sexuality. You got hard."

He pressed his body against me, and my throat caught when I felt his erection again.

"You are…hard."

"Your point?"

"How?"

He leaned over and inhaled in the space between my shoulder and my neck. "I'm not asexual, Adam. Quite the opposite. I just need a true connection before my body is interested sexually."

"And we have that connection?"

"Since we were five fucking years old, Adam. Even before I knew I wanted to kiss boys and not girls, you were the only person for me. So yeah, call it whatever you want. Friendship. Connection. We have it. My dick has no problem getting hard for you."

"How long?"

He pulled away and stared into my eyes. The green was almost black in the darkness of the hall.

"Goodnight, Adam." He pressed his lips briefly against mine, and then he was gone.

As we settled in our separate rooms, I had never been aware of a person on the other side of a wall as much as I was now. Every creak, every tiny sound grabbed my attention.

What was River doing? Jerking off? That was probably what I should do, but after confessing to him that I'd done it before, it felt wrong to do it now. Or was he replaying our kiss in his head over and over again like I was?

I was thirty years old, and kissing River was the biggest mic drop of my fucking life.

Sleep would come eventually, but for now, all I could do was lay here and think of the ways in which I wanted to change my relationship with River while simultaneously keeping it the same.

"I'm gonna get the next round. Anyone for more wings?" Adam asked.

"How is that even a question?" Noah replied, pointing at the two empty baskets.

I couldn't help stealing a glance at Adam's parting figure as he made his way through the Friday night crowd at Tanner's.

A whole week had passed since our hooky day. Seven days since the kiss, and I was going out of my mind because we'd barely spent five minutes in each other's presence.

My assistant manager, Fir, had accepted a couple of events for the restaurant, a birthday party and a retirement party. I was totally on board with those because each was an opportunity to introduce the restaurant to new clients, but they meant spending more time crunching numbers, working on staff schedules, and basically spending very little time at home.

All week, I'd envisaged bringing up the subject again with Adam because I needed to know where his head was at. But for that to happen, we had to be in the same place at the same time, which, of course, would have been tonight if I hadn't gotten a message from Lex saying they were hitting Tanner's after work.

"Adam's been a little off for a few weeks," Lex murmured, leaning in close. His twin intuition was both a blessing and a curse. "Especially this week. I found him in his office listening to music on an iPod and singing. Who the fuck even still has an iPod?"

"I don't know. I think it's kinda cute." I feigned ignorance, even as my pulse quickened. "He seems fine to me."

"Come on, River," he pressed, his concern evident. "You know him. Does he seem like himself to you?"

"He's not crying in a corner, rocking himself back and forth. Is that what you expected?"

"Well…maybe," Lex said, shooting me a knowing look, "he's acting like nothing's changed."

Lex's observation hung in the air. I raised my beer to my lips only to find it empty. The truth was, everything had changed.

The way Adam's hand had felt against my cheek, the warmth of his breath mingling with mine, the electric shock of our lips meeting…

"Let's just give him some time," I finally said, swallowing the lump in my throat.

"Time," Lex echoed, eyeing his brother across the bar. "Yeah, maybe that's exactly what he needs."

But as I caught another of Adam's fleeting looks, I couldn't shake the feeling that time was the last thing either of us truly wanted.

"Has he heard from Victoria at all?"

I shook my head.

"She needs to stay gone," Noah said. Lex elbowed him as Adam returned to the table.

"Here you go, honey," Adam said, placing a beer in front of me.

"Thank you, sweetheart," I joked. Or at least I did my best I'm-totally-joking-and-aren't-we-so-dumb impression, but I wasn't sure Noah bought it from the way his gaze ping-ponged between Adam and me.

"Anyway, I had an idea for a fundraiser for Star Finders," Adam said.

"A fundraiser?" Noah asked, his attention piqued. It was thanks to him that we learned about the Star Finders Foundation. Noah had been secretly volunteering with Drew and West for years.

It was also thanks to him and Lior that they got the lease of the old hospital building to house a youth center and shelter.

"Yeah. They desperately need help. The human power kind. It'll take them months to get the bare basics, and they're already functioning to help the local community. So, I was thinking we could help them organize an auction."

Lex laughed. "What, like a bachelor auction? They're so overdone."

"No. Well, kind of. An auction where we offer skills. Let's say Noah is up, and someone wins a bid—"

"The only person allowed to bid on and win me is Lior," he huffed.

Adam chuckled. "I think it's safe to say Lior doesn't need the skills you have to offer."

Noah's chin practically hit the floor.

"I'm talking about business. You can help someone with advice on how to start a business or make the best of networking opportunities."

"Or how to work with your family without committing murder," Noah added.

I laughed so hard it came out as a snort.

"Don't think you're getting out of it, Hartley," Adam said, elbowing me.

"What? What do I have to offer?"

His gaze softened. "You have so much to give. You run one of the busiest restaurants in the city. If nothing else, you could teach someone about time management, problem-solving, or customer service."

I kept my eyes on his, lost for words. He noticed those things? I mean, he'd worked at the restaurant growing up, just as his brothers had, but none of them wanted to make the restaurant their career. I'd thought he'd disconnected from it.

Lex grabbed his beer, tilting the lip forward. "I think it's an excellent idea. And it means we don't have to stick to single people because with everyone getting engaged and married in secret, there can't be many singles left in the city." He laughed but then stopped himself when he realized what he'd said. "Oh fuck. I'm so sorry, Adam. I didn't mean…"

Adam's earlier easy smile was replaced by a more somber expression. "I know you didn't mean it. You're right. Both you and Noah have someone. Even Tanner had a secret Vegas wedding at the same time as Noah. But I'll argue there are still plenty of single guys out there. Me, River, Drew, and West for a start."

Lex and Noah lifted their bottles, and the three brothers clinked them together.

"Oh fuck," Noah said all of a sudden. "Gotta go. We're spending the weekend at the museum house, so I have to meet Lior in his office. Tomorrow, we're having lunch with his mom, so I'll run the idea past her. She knows everyone who's anyone. We'll have a list of people to auction off skills before the end of the weekend."

"Hey, don't forget Sunday lunch at Mom and Dad's," Lex said.

"We won't be able to make it," Noah said.

"We will," Adam added. "Right, River?"

"Um…sure." Great, having dinner with the Spencer clan after kissing their straight son senseless will be super fun.

Unless I gave Fir the day off and worked instead. Adam raised his brows at me like he could tell what I was thinking.

By the time we got home, it was late, and after being up at three in the morning to go to the fish market, I could barely form a coherent thought, let alone try rehashing the kiss from a week ago.

The scent of roasting chicken and baked bread wafted through the Spencer family home as Adam and I stepped inside and were greeted by a chorus of familiar voices.

I'd been part of this family for as long as I could remember. I'd been to more Sunday lunches with the Spencers than I ever had with my mom. Because of her shift work as a nurse, we always picked a random day of the week and made it our family lunch, but while it was great to have that time with her, it lacked the loving chaos of Adam's family.

Hearing the noise of a table being set in the kitchen and Adam's mom singing to herself made me miss my mom.

A lump formed in my throat. I'd been so close to losing this. If Adam had married Victoria, she would have taken my place at the table. Not that Carla and Jack would ever not want me here. But with my strained relationship with Victoria, I wouldn't have wanted to make their family dinners awkward, which would have meant missing them more often than not.

I'd sat through a few we'd both attended and had found an excuse to leave early every single time.

"I'm going to see if your mom needs help," I said to Adam, who went straight to the living room.

"You're such a momma's boy," he teased.

"Hey, until mine returns from working abroad, I'm taking yours."

I ignored whatever he muttered and stepped into the kitchen.

"Hey, Carla."

She turned around, wiped her hands on a cloth, and reached out for a hug. "Hey, sweetheart. I'm glad you could make it. I'm making your favorite."

"Nice. Thank you. Anything I can do to help?"

"Everything's in hand. Go join the boys out there."

"River! Come here. You've got to hear this one!" Lex bellowed from the living room.

Carla shook her head. "Whatever argument they use, the answer is no. You have to back me up."

I laughed. "I got you."

Adam's laughter rang out as I slipped through the hallway into the living room.

"Dad wants to get a goat," he said.

"A goat? What for?"

Lex and Emery were cuddling in one of the armchairs, seemingly staying out of the argument.

"Hear me out," Jack said, holding his hands up. "The next-door neighbors have a micro pig. They call her Stacey. She's a terror. Whenever I turn my back on the backyard, she's there, eating my crops."

"How is getting a goat going to help? Goats eat everything."

Jack crossed his arms in front of his chest. "Yeah, and hopefully, they'll eat Stacey too."

"Dad!" Lex cried.

"Mom can't be on board with this," Adam said.

"That's where you come in. You have to convince her."

Adam's grandma came into the living room. "You're fighting a losing battle if you think Carla will ever give in on that."

"Olá, Avó," Adam said, getting up to greet her.

"Olá, Jacinta," I said, giving up my seat for her.

She raised her hand. "No need, son. Give it a second and—"

"Lunch is on the table," Carla shouted from the kitchen.

"It's like I have a little magic pinky that knows things." She winked, wiggling her pinky finger at me.

I hope your pinky finger doesn't know everything.

I followed everyone toward the kitchen until Adam grabbed my hand. "We'll be right in, Mom. I want to show River something in my bedroom."

"You know the rules," Carla said.

"If you're going to put your hands down each other's pants, don't forget to wash them after," Lex said.

"Alexis," their mom scolded.

Adam laughed. "That's the most Noah comment I've ever heard."

"He won't be missed then," Jack said. "Although he's the one who'd be on my side, I bet."

Without another word, Adam pulled me toward the hallway, past the framed photographs on the staircase wall that chronicled memories of their childhood, many of which included me. With a glance over his shoulder, he opened the door to his old bedroom.

"What are we doing here?" I asked.

Adam didn't say a word, but he locked the door and guided me to the bed.

"What—"

"Shh, don't worry, we're not having sex while my parents are downstairs."

My eyes bulged. "*That* is what you thought I was going to ask?"

He pushed me on the bed and straddled my lap. His lips curled into a defiant smile. Fuck, I wanted to kiss that cockiness off his face, but that would probably make him cockier.

"We need to talk," he said.

"I know, but this isn't the right time. Everyone's waiting for us."

"Then I guess I better make it quick."

He pressed his lips against mine, sucking them into his hot mouth. I moaned, and he took the chance to tease his tongue inside past my lips.

I kept my hands on his waist, holding on to him like I was holding on to my sanity.

He pulled away, keeping the kiss way too brief and leaving me begging for more. At least internally. Did he know what this did to me? How he was giving me a taste of something I never thought I'd try in my life?

With our chests heaving and foreheads pressed together, I wanted to stay like this forever, but the world outside the bedroom door called.

"River," Adam said, a gentle plea laden with determination. "All week, I tried to get my head around that kiss. Was it a fluke? Temporary insanity?"

"You don't look insane to me," I joked, giving up all pretense and cradling his face. "Also, that"—I pointed to where his erection pressed against mine—"doesn't look like a fluke."

He chuckled. "I guess it's happened a few times now, so I have to trust he knows what he wants."

Our eyes met again. "And that's me?"

"Yes. Don't ask me to explain it because I'm not entirely sure how we got here, but I feel like the blinders have been taken off, and now everything in my being is drawn to you."

I breathed out and leaned my head against his chest. He threaded his fingers through my hair.

"Don't break my heart, Adam."

He kissed me again, this time with the kind of reverence that made me wish his family would disappear into thin air so we could stay here forever.

"Come on, let's have some food and then go home. I'd like to spend the rest of the afternoon naked."

20

ADAM

"ADAM? RIVER?" My mom's voice sliced through the fog of desire clouding my thoughts as we joined the family around the large kitchen table. "What took you boys so long?"

River's cheeks flushed pink as he took his usual seat next to mine. My breath almost caught at how adorable he looked like that. How had I never noticed?

"We had a bet about my Ninja Turtle sticker collection," I said, flashing a grin. "Had to prove I still had them all."

Lex raised an eyebrow but held his tongue. It's not like he'd know *exactly* what we'd been up to in the bedroom, right?

And if he did, it's not like he'd say anything because more than once since he'd found Emery again, I'd heard moans coming from his old bedroom before or after Sunday lunch. Noah too.

I never used to understand it because there was no way Victoria would have gone up to my room to make out with my whole family downstairs. I used to think it was a respect thing, but I knew how much Emery and Lior loved and respected my parents.

The truth was that what Victoria and I had hadn't included that raw desperation to touch each other at all times. A feeling I was starting to get acquainted with because my hands itched to touch River now.

Throughout the meal, I barely enjoyed the food. Every bite was as delicious as every other meal we'd had at my mom's hands, but it was nothing compared to the anticipation I felt for what came after the meal.

Each time River reached for his glass, his shirt sleeve rubbed against mine and sent a jolt through my body, a reminder of the electrifying kiss we'd shared moments before.

Even the way he licked his dessert spoon had me thinking of other things he could do with that tongue.

Dammit, I shouldn't have been looking at gay porn last night.

I'd read many of River's spicy romance novels, so I wasn't completely unaware of how sex between two men worked. Now, thinking back, maybe the way I'd gotten aroused by some of the scenes I'd read since River had gotten me hooked on male-male romance was a giveaway. What straight man reads gay romance, gets aroused during the spicy scenes, *and* still thinks they're straight?

Yeah, there's amazing writing talent, and there's burying your head in the sand.

I was such a dumbass.

When everybody finished their dessert, I stood up, impatient to escape, and met River's gaze across the table. "Thanks for lunch, Mom. I'll help you clear up."

This time, Emery looked at me like I'd grown a second head, swiftly joined by my mom, who stopped midway through clearing a plate.

Come on. It's not like it's the first time I've ever offered to help clear the table.

"What?" I asked innocently.

"Nothing, sweetie." Her gaze flickered between River and me.

I ignored it and started filling the dishwasher before running the water to clean the big pots.

Lex and Emery joined in and Dad took River into his office to talk about the restaurant, as usual. Before long, the kitchen was sparkly clean, and my mom looked worried that she'd stepped into an alternate dimension.

"Lex, do you think we should be offended that Mom is in shock because we helped?" I asked my brother.

He laughed. "To be fair, as soon as Emery starts helping, we all run to the living room. I felt guilty today."

Mom walked up and squished us between her arms.

"Ew, what's this? Affection? Lex, make it stop."

"You can complain all you want, but I'll never stop loving and hugging my boys any chance I get."

Dad and River came into the kitchen, witnessing the cuddle assault.

"Oh no, now she's gonna want to bake," Dad said before going toward the living room.

"Now that's an idea," Mom said.

"Actually," I said, meeting River's eyes. "We should probably head out."

Mom sighed. "Okay. You boys work too much. In my day, Sunday was Sunday."

Lex rolled his eyes and I just smiled. Mom was such a liar. Every Sunday for as long as we can remember was spent at the restaurant. This Sunday lunch business only started once my parents handed over the running of the restaurant to River.

"Thanks for lunch, Carla. It was delicious as always," River said before giving my mom a hug.

"Be safe, boys," Mom called out when we were almost by the car.

"Oh, we will," I shouted back without taking my eyes off River, whose face reddened again.

"I'm gonna kill you," he whispered over the roof of my car.

"As long as you do it with your dick, we're good."

I got in the driver's seat and purposefully didn't look at him.

"How are you so okay with this?" he asked.

"Fake it 'til you make it?" I shrugged.

"I'm serious. I—"

I reached over and placed my hand on his leg. "I know what I want, River. If you need some convincing, I'm happy to show you as soon as we're indoors."

He groaned but didn't say anything for the rest of the drive.

When the door to his place swung shut behind us, River's hands were on me instantly, his fingers threading through my hair as he pulled me into him. My back hit the wall with a soft thud, and I was suddenly acutely aware of every place where our bodies touched. The warmth of his palms seeped through the fabric of my shirt, heating my already scorched skin.

"Are you sure this is what you want?" he murmured against my ear.

I wanted to laugh, to tell him my entire being was screaming yes, but words seemed inadequate. Instead, I let my body speak for me, pressing into his. He couldn't deny an erection, could he?

In response, River's mouth captured mine. I surrendered to the kiss like prey willingly walking into the predator's lair.

"You drive me fucking insane, Adam." He ran his teeth over my jaw and my whole body trembled. "Do you have any idea of how much I want you?"

"We could have gotten here earlier if you'd helped in the kitchen."

He pressed me harder against the wall. "You think you're funny. Let's see if you're such a smartass when you're naked with another man."

"You say that like I don't know exactly who I'm going to be naked with, which brings me to the point. I need us to be wearing less clothes. A lot less clothes."

River's fingers entwined with mine as he dragged me down the hallway. Our socked feet were slippery on the hardwood floor. I laughed as River nearly slipped before the same thing happened to me.

Lightness. My whole life was about words, and that one was all I could feel. Even as I crossed the bridge into a new me, I was light, so when the scent of his cologne and body wash assaulted my senses as he opened the door, my belly tightened and my chest expanded.

"We'll take it slow, okay?" he said softly as he led me to the edge of his bed.

I nodded, my throat closing up all of a sudden. God, I wanted this so much. His hands on me, his mouth on me. I wanted to feel the weight of his body on top of mine. I wanted everything but didn't know how to ask for it.

"Is...is it possible to feel so much that you freeze?" I asked, finding my voice.

River pulled my hands to ask me to sit down and then knelt between my thighs, his eyes never leaving mine. I opened my legs to accommodate him.

"I am very familiar with the concept."

He grabbed the hem of my shirt and pulled it over my head. His mouth pressed against my sternum with a soft kiss. More followed as he peppered my chest with kisses, leaving a trail of fire with each one.

"That feels good."

I reached for his shirt and he leaned back, removing it for me. My mouth watered at the sight of his chest, the tattoos, the chest hair that was darker than the hair on his head.

"You're so beautiful, River. I love your tattoos."

His gaze met mine and he shook his head like he didn't believe the words out of my mouth.

He undid his jeans and pulled them down with his underwear. I gasped at the sight of his hard cock. I'd only ever seen it covered by the fabric of his underwear or a towel.

His eyes were full of vulnerability as he pushed his clothes away.

I unzipped my pants and did the same until we were both naked.

"Scoot up," he said. I moved to the middle of the bed. My dick pointed up, leaving no doubt about where this was headed.

I gasped when River followed me onto the middle of the bed, covered my body with his, and our dicks touched.

Sexuality was a spectrum. I'd believed that since Noah had come out to the family as pansexual, and now, with River's cock touching mine, there was no shadow of a doubt that I was not and probably had never been straight.

"What do you want to happen here, Adam?"

"Is everything too much to ask?"

He chuckled. "I'm going to manage your expectations here. It's been a long time since I've had sex that didn't involve my hand. This might be over embarrassingly quick."

"I'm not worried about your staying power. It's your refractory period I want to test."

"You're on," he said, a glint of his competitive side showing in his eyes. "Can I suck you?"

"Like I'm going to say no to that."

His mouth moved lower, kissing down my neck, my

chest, until I was gasping, lost in the haze of pleasure as he took me in his mouth.

There was no easing me into it. He took my cock right down until it hit the back of his throat. He sucked hard on the way up before repeating it a million times.

"Oh my, fucking—argh, River!" I cried, the suction driving me crazy. Every stroke, every flick of his tongue, unraveled me from the inside out. I was so close.

"River," I gasped, and there was a plea in my voice that I couldn't have held back if I tried.

"Come in my mouth."

"Are you sure?" I'd never had a girlfriend who'd wanted that, so I'd always thought cum didn't taste very nice.

"I need it. Please, Adam."

I nodded, and he resumed his assault. With one hand around the base of my cock he sucked harder around the head. My elbows slipped on the sheets and I fell on my back. River never stopped.

"I'm coming," I shouted as my whole body locked and I spilled weeks of pent-up desire down his throat.

River sucked me until there was nothing left.

I reached for him, my hands trembling as I tried to find a tiny ounce of energy.

He lay beside me, his hard cock pressing against my thigh.

"That was—" he started.

"Perfect, River. Utter perfection."

He placed his hand on my chest, over my fast-beating heart.

"Let me take care of you," I said, my eyes closed as I fought the need to drift off. There was no way I was going to be a selfish partner. River deserved more than that.

I trailed a pattern down his side until my hand circled his

cock. It was thick and heavy. Not so different from mine, but it was longer. I wondered how it would feel inside me.

"I'm not fucking you tonight," he said.

My chin dropped. "How did you know what I was thinking?"

He raised a brow. "I didn't, but I know you like to throw yourself headfirst into a challenge."

I closed my hand around his cock and twisted on an upward move.

River gasped as I chuckled. "You were saying about me throwing myself in head first?"

As I explored further, his breath hitched, his lean muscles tensing. I sped up the strokes, and his response was immediate, a sharp intake of breath that became a moan. With each stroke, I learned what made his body sing until he was teetering on the edge, held there by the thread of my touch.

The sounds out of his beautiful lips got me hard again, so I pressed closer against him and took both our cocks in my hand. I knew I wouldn't come again, but I hoped the friction would get him there.

"I'm so cl—Adam!" he shouted as his release coated my fingers, warm and sticky.

Afterward, we lay there, limbs entangled, River's chest rising and falling against my side.

"You fucking bastard," he said, reaching for my hand, our fingers intertwining naturally.

"I take it that was okay."

"That was more than okay," he whispered, each syllable heavy with meaning. "You have no idea how scarily more than okay this was for me."

My chest filled with pride and hope. If us being together like this was more than okay for River, that was because we had a true connection. Not just the best friend kind of connection, but the kind like what my brothers had.

I tried to look for the fear in my head, but I must have misplaced it somewhere outside River's apartment because all I could feel was rightness.

21

———

RIVER

I STOOD motionless in the storeroom, my hand hovering over a crate of lemons. I'd forgotten what they were for as I replayed it all again—the warmth of Adam's touch, the unexpected connection between us that had surged like a live wire, the rightness I felt being with him.

It was ludicrous that Adam, my childhood friend, the same man with those piercing blue eyes that never seemed to hold anything but brotherly affection for me, had sought my touch like he was craving it more than his next breath.

I could still feel the roughness of his breath against my skin, every whispered word, every moan.

Disbelief didn't quite describe my emotional state of mind. I'd accepted years ago that what I felt for Adam was more than friendship. I knew the exact moment I stopped seeing Adam as the kid from school with the blond straggly hair and started seeing him as a man. Noticed every single curve on his body, the way he pronounced certain words, or how he smelled.

We'd been fourteen, and I'd said yes to the kiss that had sealed my fate.

159

But the way my body reacted to his touch? I didn't want to believe how deep it reached.

"River?" The chef's voice cut through my reverie, sharp and impatient. "We needed those lemons ten minutes ago!"

"Sorry," I muttered, finally grabbing a handful of the fruit. I gave a passing server the lemons and asked him to take them to the chef. If my time in hospitality had taught me anything, it was to stay out of the way of a crabby chef, and while ours was generally a great guy, he didn't like to be kept waiting when he had work to do.

I slipped unseen to the front of the house, something I regretted immediately.

Drew's complex moves with a cocktail glass hid how good he was at picking up social cues, which was why I'd tried to avoid him since he started his shift today. But I knew it was only a matter of time until he trapped me.

"Hey," Drew said, his voice low enough not to carry, "everything okay with you tonight?"

I nodded, forcing my gaze toward the happy diners in the restaurant. "Yeah, just tired is all."

"Uh-huh," Drew replied, clearly unconvinced but respecting the boundary. "Fundraiser planning is going wild," he added. "West is on a roll."

"Really? That's great. Will you tell me if you guys need any help?"

He gave me a *sure* before his lips curled into a smile. "You have company."

I looked toward the restaurant door, my breath catching.

"So, you're *just* tired, huh?" Drew muttered before Adam reached us, a hesitant smile on his lips.

"Hey, I thought I'd grab something to eat," Adam said, placing his hands in the pockets of his jeans. "I didn't feel like cooking."

"Sure," I exhaled. "You could have called. You know we deliver."

"Sometimes," he started, edging closer to the counter where I stood frozen, "you don't know what you want until you see it."

I had to bite my tongue to stop from reacting and giving myself away. Drew was extremely good at pretending he was doing something else when his entire focus was on something happening yards away. The man was the velociraptor of bartenders.

"And what are you in the mood for?" I managed to say, my voice steadier than I felt.

"Can I have the house steak? I'm in the mood for good quality meat."

Drew snorted, so I grabbed Adam by the hand and led him to my office.

"Steak isn't the kind of food you have delivered," I said as the door clicked shut behind us. "If you're a steak connoisseur, of course."

Adam leaned back against my solid oak desk, his blue eyes dark with something that sent a shiver down my spine and made my underwear feel way too tight.

"River," he said, his voice low and certain, pulling me into his orbit.

"Adam," I began as I stepped forward, closing the gap with a resolve I hadn't known I possessed. I got close enough that I could smell his body wash. Or, more precisely, *my* body wash. Fucker had been home and showered using my soap again.

Our lips met, the kiss an inevitable explosion I was starting to believe was the result of this constant spark between us.

Hands roamed, exploring now-familiar terrain. Clothes

got in the way, but I wasn't so far gone that I couldn't keep ahold of myself. There were lines we couldn't cross.

"God, River," Adam murmured against his skin, "You drive me crazy—"

"And I'm crazy for you," I confessed, my breath hitching as Adam's mouth found the sensitive spot just below my ear.

I reluctantly pulled back. The longer we stayed here, the more likely someone would walk in on us.

"I'll wait up for you tonight," he said, his gaze searching mine.

"Tonight?"

"Yeah," he said, a smile playing on his lips. "When you're done here, come home. I'll wait up."

"Okay." I cradled his face, smiling as he closed his eyes and leaned into my touch.

"Let me get your order ready. What do you really want to eat?"

"I've already had dinner," he replied casually.

I shook my head. "You're cunning."

"But I got to kiss you," he said, holding my gaze a moment longer than necessary. "See you later?"

"Later." I leaned against the desk as I watched him exit my office. I needed an extra couple of minutes to pull myself together.

Drew hit me with a knowing look, shook his head slightly, and returned to his tasks when I walked past the bar later. I ignored him. One day he'd have a taste of his own medicine because I was absolutely sure it was only a matter of time until the dam broke and Drew's and West's feelings for each other spilled out.

I spent the rest of the night helping between stations and talking to customers. I truly loved my job despite the long hours, and tonight's constant stream of walk-ins and bookings was the perfect distraction from thoughts of Adam at home waiting for me.

He often read late into the night, although I'd never seen the light in his bedroom on when I came home after closing the restaurant, so I wondered if today would be different.

As soon as I stepped into the dimly lit hallway of my apartment, my belly sank a little. It was coming up on one in the morning, so I shouldn't be surprised to find my place as quiet as it usually was at this time.

In the living room, the moonlight filtered through the blinds, casting long shadows over the furniture. No signs of an Adam that had stayed up late reading on the couch and then fallen asleep.

I made my way down the small hallway. His bedroom door was closed. I shouldn't be disappointed, but it was a sign that I'd already allowed Adam to burrow too deep inside my heart. I couldn't help the feeling.

Bypassing my room, I went straight to the bathroom and took a quick shower to get ready for bed. I'd never had to worry about moving around my place late at night, but since Adam moved in, I'd been more mindful of the noise because the bathroom was right across from his bedroom.

But as I walked past the threshold of my bedroom, there Adam was, sprawled across my bed, a peaceful expression softening his features.

He must have dozed off while waiting.

I leaned against the doorframe, arms crossed, taking in the scene I'd so often imagined but never thought would happen. Adam's chest rose and fell with the slow cadence of deep sleep, his breaths quiet whispers in the darkened room.

There was a book on the floor where his hand hung off the bed.

With careful movements, I sat on the edge of the bed,

the mattress dipping slightly under my weight. Adam stirred, a soft sigh escaping him, but he did not wake.

I slid under the covers, leaving a gap between us. Sleeping in the same bed was getting into even more dangerous territory than kissing or having sex, but after having a small taste of Adam, I couldn't stop myself from wanting the whole thing.

I slid forward, ever so slightly, bridging the gap between us. At the same time, Adam shifted in his sleep as though he knew I was there. His back nestled against my chest, so I draped my arm around him, pulling him closer still.

I closed my eyes and breathed in the familiar scent that clung to Adam before placing a soft kiss on the back of his neck.

As sleep claimed me, I allowed myself to pretend this was my new future. Adam and I together, sharing a bed, waking up to each other every morning.

22

ADAM

CLUTCHING a box of Kleenex like a life raft, I lay sprawled beneath a tangle of blankets, feeling every inch the pathetic sight I must have presented. The tickle at the back of my throat was a constant reminder, not that I needed one, of the minor cold that had taken up residence in my sinuses.

I heard the door click open and closed with the familiar sound of River's return. I wanted to greet him at the door, pull him in, and push him against the wall, kissing him senseless. Instead, I was a soggy vegetable with no energy.

"Hey," River called out as he entered the living room, his voice carrying the soft edges of concern. His eyes found me on the couch, an expression of wry sympathy crossing his face.

"Hey," I managed, my words muffled by congestion. "Sorry for the biohazard zone."

River chuckled, taking a seat on the edge of the couch.

"Doesn't look like you've got a fever," he observed, pressing the back of his hand against my forehead. "Probably just a twenty-four-hour thing."

"Thanks, Dr. Hartley," I joked weakly, grateful for his lack of hesitation, even in the face of my germy state.

"Always here for you, Adam," he replied, sincerity threaded through his gentle tone.

I shifted slightly, trying to find a more comfortable position without losing the warmth River brought into the room. The familiar scent of Lusitana clung to him—a mixture of spices and comfort that had come to signify home in my mind.

"Mind if I join your infirmary?" he asked, already sliding closer until his thigh pressed reassuringly against mine.

"Your funeral," I teased, though the fondness in my voice betrayed my true feelings. River's willingness to brave the snotty trenches with me was just another piece of evidence in the growing case of how much he meant to me.

He settled in next to me, careful not to jostle me too much as he draped an arm around my shoulders. "I'll take my chances."

In silence, we sank into the cushions, the hum of the outside world fading. It was these moments—quiet, unassuming—that made me wonder just how deep my feelings for River ran.

"Thanks for being here," I whispered after a while.

"Wouldn't be anywhere else," River murmured, his fingertips absently tracing patterns on the blanket that covered us both.

"Let's order dinner from that Thai place you love. What sounds good?" River asked, his voice a balm to the racket of sniffles and coughs that had been my symphony since morning.

"Pad See Ew," I croaked, the mere thought of wide noodles and savory sauce enough to make me forget the relentless tickle in my throat. "And we need Tom Kha Gai. Its magic could probably cure this cold."

"Ah, the healing powers of coconut soup," River chuckled, his thumbs deftly navigating the screen on his phone as he placed the order. "I should've guessed you'd go for the comfort foods."

"You remember that time you tried the Evil Jungle Prince curry?" I teased, a smile tugging at my lips despite the persistent stuffiness in my head. "Your face matched your shirt. I wasn't sure if it was a fashion statement or a cry for help."

River laughed, the sound rich and warm. "That was nothing compared to your culinary masterpiece during finals week. The 'Spaghetti a la Adam'—burned to perfection."

"Hey, that was art. Abstract cuisine." My defense was halfhearted, but the memory sparked a lightness in my chest.

"All right, food is ordered," he said, setting his phone aside. "Now we just wait for the magic soup to work its wonders."

"Thank you," I whispered, gratitude mingling with a thousand other unspoken emotions.

"Anytime."

I caught myself gazing at him longer than necessary, lost in the way his laughter softened the lines around his eyes.

"River," I began, my voice barely above a whisper. The words tumbled out before I could stop them. "I want to kiss you so bad right now, but I can't even breathe through my nose."

His expression shifted, a playful smirk giving way to something more tender, more cautious. "I'd rather remain germ-free, thanks." He winked, but there was a hesitation in his voice that let me know my confession hadn't fallen on deaf ears.

"Sorry," I mumbled, looking away. "Cold meds talking."

"Don't apologize," River said, his voice low, serious. "It's not the cold meds, Adam. It's us. This thing between us."

My heart skipped a beat, my eyes snapping back to his. "Thing?"

"Whatever it is," he said, shrugging slightly, but his gaze held mine with an intensity that sent shivers down my spine.

"Is it weird?" I asked, my insecurities bubbling to the surface.

"Nothing about this is weird," River reassured me, his hand finding mine beneath the blanket, giving it a gentle squeeze. "It's just…new territory. For both of us."

"New territory."

"Exactly," he said, the corner of his mouth lifting in a half-smile that made my heart race. "And I think it's worth exploring."

"Even with my germs?" I teased, trying to lighten the mood.

"Even with your germs," he confirmed, his thumb brushing against the back of my hand in a gesture that felt like a promise.

"Good," I said, feeling a resolve settle over me. "Because once I'm better, I plan on taking you up on that."

River's smile grew wider, and he leaned back against the couch, pulling me with him. "I'll hold you to that."

I found comfort in the weight of his arm around my shoulders, the silent conversations we held with our eyes, and the undeniable truth that we were on the brink of something beautiful.

The doorbell's chime sliced through the comfortable silence, and River was on his feet before my brain could register the sound as the arrival of our Thai feast. He returned with bags that filled the room with the rich, tempting aroma of spices and herbs. My stomach growled in anticipation, echoing louder than my sniffles.

"Here we go, my dear patient," River announced, setting

the spread out on the coffee table. "Feast your eyes and your taste buds on this."

"God, it looks amazing," I managed between coughs, sitting up to help him unpack containers of delicious food. The steamy warmth wafting from the dishes seemed almost medicinal, and I breathed it in, hoping for a momentary reprieve from my congestion.

With dinner sorted, River browsed through the streaming service for a movie, settling on a romantic comedy with two male leads.

"Perfect choice," I approved, my voice rougher than I liked.

"Thought you'd say that."

As characters flitted across the screen, I found myself watching River, the way his lips quirked at a joke as he chewed the delicious food, or when he stopped with his food mid-air because the main characters almost kissed.

I couldn't finish all my food, but I already felt so much better having eaten something.

When he finished, River resumed his place on the couch behind me. I closed my eyes, relishing the feel of his arms around me and the warmth of the blanket. If I wasn't careful, I'd fall asleep on him.

"You know, if I had a superpower," he said, his breath a warm whisper against my ear, "it'd be to make clothes fold themselves."

"Because that's what the world needs," I retorted, stifling a yawn, "a laundry-themed superhero."

"Hey, don't mock the small conveniences," he shot back, his tone indignant. "Next, you'll tell me you wouldn't want a power to never lose your keys again."

"Touché."

River's hand found mine, fingers intertwining naturally.

"Sometimes I think…" His voice trailed off, hesitant.

"Think what?" I asked, turning my head slightly to look at him. His eyes were a soft green in the low light, reflective pools that seemed to hold entire galaxies.

"Never mind. It's nothing." His gaze dropped, focusing on where our hands were joined.

"Tell me," I urged gently, squeezing his hand. "Please."

He sighed, a sound filled with a lifetime of longing and restraint. "I just... I cherish this. Us. I always have."

"Me too, River." The admission came easily because it was the purest truth I knew. In all my past relationships, I'd never felt the kind of peace I did with him, never experienced such a harmonious intermingling of souls.

"Whatever happens," he began, his voice a steady stream threading through the silence, "I want you to know that this, what we have, whatever it is, means everything to me."

"River, I—" Emotion swelled in my throat, thickening my words. "It means everything to me too. More than I ever thought."

23

RIVER

LYING THERE, with the morning light coming through the partially open curtains, I watched Adam breathe. There was something sacred in the stillness of watching someone sleep, something intimate and rare. I let myself get lost in it—his chest rising and falling with a rhythm that relaxed my worried heart.

I remembered the panic that had gripped me days ago when his fever spiked. Twenty-four-hour thing, my ass. But now, the worry lines that had etched themselves across my forehead smoothed away as I saw no trace of sickness on his serene face. His skin was free of that unnatural heat, his breaths deep and even.

He seemed so at peace. A stray lock of his dirty-blond hair fell across his forehead, and I resisted the urge to reach out and brush it aside to feel the warmth of his skin under my fingertips.

I propped myself up on one elbow, careful not to jostle the bed, but the vibration of my phone broke the stillness in the room. *Mom* flashed on the screen, reminding me I hadn't called her as I'd promised myself I would.

"Sorry," I whispered, as much to Adam as to myself, before tapping the screen and bringing the phone to my ear.

"Morning, Mom," I said, my voice hushed.

She launched into her usual inquiries, and I found myself caught between the desire to share everything and the fear of saying too much. As I spoke, my gaze lingered on Adam, drinking in the sight of him, the reality.

"Everything's fine," I assured her, and it was true, in a way. Adam's recovery was a relief that settled warm in my chest.

"River, are you sure?" she pressed, her maternal instincts attuned to the nuances in my voice.

"Positive," I replied. "How about you?"

"It's been great here, but I'm getting antsy and homesick. I think I'm going to end the contract here and come home. My old boss has been pestering me to return to the hospital."

I smiled wide as though she could see me. "Are you serious, Mom?"

"Yeah. I miss you a lot too. Working abroad was something I needed to do, you know? But it's time to come home."

"I get it, Mom. You needed to experience life outside of being a working single mom."

She chuckled. "You were a good kid, but yeah, your dad dying so young changed the plans we had as a family. Never got to give you a baby brother or sister."

Her voice was strained, as it always was when she mentioned my dad.

"I have my bonus family, Mom. You know I've never missed not having a sibling. Adam, Lex, and Noah more than made up for it," I chuckled.

"Speaking of which, how is he?"

I sighed. My mom, with her infinite mom instinct, or maybe it was because she was a nurse and could smell bullshit a mile away, had known I had a crush on Adam since I was sixteen. She'd gone into protective bear-mom mode because, at that time, there had been no indication Adam was anything but straight, and she didn't want me to get my heart broken.

By then, it had been too late. The kiss had happened, and my fate had been sealed. Not that I'd known at the time. My demisexuality didn't become apparent to me until I was in college and learned more about queer identities.

"He's…okay. He's staying here until he gets back on his feet."

"River…"

"Don't worry, Mom. I'm okay."

Adam stirred, and then his eyes fluttered open. When he saw me, he smiled and reached out for me.

Yeah, I was more than okay.

"Listen, Mom, I have to get ready for work."

"Okay, honey. Look after yourself."

"You too, Mom. And I want to hear more about your plans soon."

"Sure thing."

I put the phone away and turned back to Adam.

"Morning, sleepyhead." I pushed his messy hair off his forehead.

"Morning. Did I stir much last night?" he asked.

"No. You slept like a baby." I gave him a soft kiss on the lips. "But you snored like a truck."

"I did not!"

I laughed at his indignation. "You're right, you didn't. It was more like a small locomotive. For a moment there, I thought I'd have to call the Department of Transportation to ask for a fault assessment."

I was still laughing when, all of a sudden, I found myself under Adam with my hands pinned over my head.

"I see you regained your strength."

"I had a good nurse."

He ran his nose over the side of my face and then sucked my skin until I knew there would be a mark later. My dick hardened immediately.

"Feels like my nurse is ready for the morning round."

I growled, and holding his hands tight, I raised my head to kiss him. He met my lips with the usual need. Adam always gave everything in a kiss. It was a long way away from the inexperienced kiss we'd shared at fourteen.

Adam's tongue caressed mine as he gave himself to the kiss. His hips were doing a job on my poor rock-hard dick.

"Hmm, Adam…"

"I missed you," he said into my lips, giving me no opportunity to mirror the words. I'd have to show him instead.

Releasing his hands, I flipped us until I was the one on top.

"Do you know what the time is, Adam?" I asked as he chased my lips.

"Don't care."

I chuckled.

"I'll tell you then. It's time for you to decide whether you're going back to work or staying in bed another day."

He groaned. "I can't stay home another day. I'll go mad."

"Besides, you've already gone through all the episodes of *Golden Girls*."

"Yup."

"Okay, let's go shower then because I have a couple of meetings today."

I laughed when he pouted. "But, River…" He canted his hips against mine like I couldn't already feel his erection.

"Yes, Adam?" I stood up from the bed, and he followed me as I walked backward out of the bedroom and into the bathroom.

"Can I give you a hand job?" he asked.

I shook my head.

"Blowjob?"

I shook my head again and then turned the water on. When it was at the correct temperature, I pulled him inside with me. His eyes shone like two blue marbles as I caged him against the wall.

"I'm going to suck you until you come because you've been such a good patient, and then you're going to take my dick in your hand and stroke it until I paint your body with my cum."

"Fuck—"

"I'm not done. And when we're both nice and clean, I'm going to make you breakfast. You're going to eat all of it because while you think you're well enough to go to work, I know you'll probably try to catch up with everything in one day, and you'll forget to eat."

He closed his eyes and bit his lower lip. "I'm not sure which of those things is making my dick harder."

I went down on my knees and sucked his dick until he spilled down my throat.

The time it took him to recover from his orgasm was a testament to how he still wasn't fully recovered, so even though he did stroke me until I came all over him, I was glad he'd agreed to stay home long enough to have breakfast.

"Hey," he said as I opened the front door when we were both leaving for work. "Thank you for looking after me."

"You already thanked me in the shower." I winked.

"You know what I mean."

I pulled him by the front of his coat until he was close enough for me to circle my arms around his waist. I caressed his cheek and said, "I'm closing for the next couple of nights."

He nodded.

"Will you be in my bed when I come home?"

His smile and the way he grabbed my face to kiss me were all the confirmation I needed.

Maybe also the confirmation that Adam was getting in as deep as I already was.

24

———

ADAM

I stood over my desk, dozens of sticky notes with scribbled words making a word cloud of emotions, textures, and visual cues.

My brainstorming strategy had worked for me from college to this day. I paced the room, wrote down words, listened to one of the many playlists River had created for me over the years, and let my creativity do the rest.

Maybe I was coming down with a cold again, or something, because I couldn't focus for shit. I glanced at the clock, a mild panic rushing over me as I realized I needed to come up with three more copy options for the campaign we were building for a local fashion brand before my meeting with Lex and Noah in a few hours.

Lex had done his thing and come up with the perfect design. Now it was my turn.

Maybe I could run it by the team. We usually worked together, but there were a few occasions when clients wanted to work with Lex and me directly.

Our team was busy enough, and it was fun working with Lex to create something really special for our clients. It was like going back to the early days when there was no one but us and Noah, and we all worked in a tiny shared office.

"Hey." Lex's voice cut through my distraction as he stepped into my office. "You've been staring at that desk for ages. Everything okay?"

"Must be nice having the time to stare across the room into my office for something to do."

He sat on the small leather couch I'd bought so I wasn't always working at my desk.

"What can I say? Staring at you is just a reminder of how gorgeous I am."

"I didn't think you had self-confidence issues. Not when Emery won't stop looking at you like you put the stars in the sky and flipped a switch to turn on the moon."

Lex smiled, his expression softening the way it did every time Emery came up in conversation. He studied me for a moment longer than necessary, then asked, "You okay, man?"

"Yeah, I'm fine." The lie tasted bitter on my tongue, but I wasn't ready to unpack the tangled mess of my feelings—not even with Lex, who knew me better than anyone. "Just… trying to nail this copy. It's giving me a hard time."

"All right," Lex said, though his eyes lingered with unspoken questions. "If you say so. Just remember, I'm here if you need to talk."

"I know." I managed a weak smile.

Being a twin was the best thing ever. The bond I shared with Lex was unbreakable and special. But I hadn't believed Lex when he said he'd bumped into Emery after a year apart and that Emery had been in an accident and lost his memory.

When my brother's reaction to my engagement had been somewhere between lukewarm and hostile, I didn't consider that maybe they saw something in Victoria I'd missed or refused to see.

So how could I trust myself and the newly growing feelings for River but also explain the chaos in my head?

How could I tell Lex that every moment spent with River lately felt like stepping into a new world, where the blinders had come off and I was suddenly seeing everything in bright colors? How I craved his company, his touch, and just sitting beside him watching a movie made me feel so much happier than I'd ever been with the woman I thought I'd loved enough to marry?

How was it possible that I had once been so certain about marrying Victoria but now questioned everything?

When I thought of River, I lost my breath, my heart beat faster, I craved his smell, his smile, even his laugh.

Was this the shape of love? Or just lust cloaked in the sheen of novelty?

"Adam, I've just watched you go through five hundred different moods, and you forgot I was still here. Care to stop bullshitting the bullshitter? Remember, I was the master of 'I'm fine' for a whole year."

"I'm—I don't know what you want me to say."

He leaned forward on the couch and rested his elbows on his knees. "I don't want you to tell me what you think I want to hear."

I exhaled slowly. "I just wish everyone would stop asking if I'm okay," I admitted, averting my gaze from his probing eyes. "It's like I've become the family project."

Lex crossed his arms, a knowing smile playing at the corners of his mouth. "Maybe when I see you behaving like you used to—full of life and less…broody—I'll stop asking."

I wanted to argue, to tell him I was the same old Adam, but the words wouldn't come out. Probably because I wasn't the same old Adam. I'd changed, and I didn't fully understand it yet, so how could I explain it to someone else?

"Is this about Victoria?" Lex's voice softened, the mention of her name like a knife twisting in my gut.

"No, she hasn't been in touch. She's still gone. And since I'm no longer at the apartment, I wouldn't know if she's back."

"How is it living with River again?" It was a seemingly innocent question, but Lex was way too perceptive, especially when it came to me.

"River's… It's good," I began, the words faltering as they escaped. "It's comfortable, you know? Like old times." But even as I said it, I could tell Lex knew I was leaving a lot unsaid.

"Are you thinking about looking for your own place soon?"

I walked over to the window and stared at the street outside. "I'll start looking eventually." The thought had crossed my mind a few times, but each time, the need to be close to River won out. Even when I didn't see him, I knew he was there. Waking up before me, coming home after a late shift and joining me in his bed.

This couldn't be all about the physical aspect. Not when I only ever properly drifted off to sleep when River's arm pulled me against his chest and his hand sought mine.

"Okay. Well then, I better leave you and your sticky notes alone."

I sighed. Yeah, I better go back to the sticky notes.

An hour and a lot of frustration later, I'd made some progress, but now my belly was rumbling.

A knock on the door made me look up and put a smile on my face.

"River."

"Hey," he said, his lips widening into a grin that reached his beautiful eyes and made the butterflies in my head all fluttery.

"What are you doing here?" I stood and walked to him, stopping short when I realized I'd been about to kiss him right in the middle of my office where everyone could see.

"You've never asked that before."

"Sorry. I didn't mean that quite the way it came out. I just wasn't expecting you today."

"I was in the area to see the restaurant accountant and thought you might need a pick-me-up," he said, handing me the coffee and pastry bag in his hand.

"Thank you." I took my gifts and sipped the coffee straight away. "Hmm, you have no idea how much I needed this. I was actually about to pop out to buy myself a coffee."

"I'm glad you didn't, or I'd have missed you."

I put the coffee on my desk. "Is that something you do a lot? Miss me?"

His warm gaze washed over me like he wanted to do more than just look. "More and more each day. I curse the distance between the restaurant and your office, my long hours, and having to leave you asleep in my bed when all I want is to kiss you awake."

I closed my eyes and took a deep breath, muttering, "My office is see-through," more to remind myself why I couldn't just push him onto the couch and make out for the rest of the afternoon.

"You look stuck," he said, pointing at the work on my desk.

"It's for a fashion brand. I'm supposed to conjure up the next big slogan, but nothing feels right."

"Let's hear it then," River said, easing onto the chair across from me. We'd done this so many times I'd lost count. He had a talent for picking up on a loose thread and giving me exactly what I needed to create the perfect slogan or ad copy.

I rattled off a couple of attempts I'd scribbled down earlier, each falling flat the moment they left my lips.

"Okay, how about this?" he said, leaning forward with a spark of excitement. "What if we infuse the idea with taste? Everyone loves food, right? When you make that sensory association, it doesn't matter what you're selling. People will remember it."

"Go on," I urged, sensing we were on the cusp of something brilliant.

"Think about it. The brand isn't just selling clothes. It's selling an experience. An indulgence." His voice dropped to a near whisper. "Like that first bite of something exquisite that you'll never forget."

"An experience that lingers on your palate," I murmured, my mind spinning with possibilities. "A taste of luxury you can't forget." I looked up at him, and our eyes met in a shared moment of triumph.

He sat back on the chair, stealing a bite of the pastry he bought for me. "I'm a fucking genius."

"You should be doing my job."

"Ah, but your job doesn't come with a chef," he teased back, his eyes flickering with that playful spark that always seemed to ignite something warm in me.

The office air hung thick with unspoken words as we smiled at each other. I fucking wanted to kiss him so bad. More than kiss him. I wanted to touch him and watch him unravel at my hands just like he'd been doing every time we had more than five minutes together at home.

Leaning over the desk, River brought himself as close as propriety would allow, those beautiful eyes holding mine in a silent conversation.

"I should get back to the restaurant," he said, breaking the spell.

"Okay." I tried to hide my disappointment but failed miserably

"Saturday," River continued, "keep it open."

"Oh yeah? You want to take me out on a date?" I teased.

"As a matter of fact, yes."

The thought of spending an entire day with River set my pulse racing.

"Okay, I'll make sure I'm ready for you," I managed, my voice steady despite the implicit confession.

He winked and then left me in my office with an inconvenient erection and five minutes to go before a meeting with my brothers.

25

RIVER

MY BELLY CLENCHED as a wave of pleasure struck me. For a moment, I was lost in the haze of sleep, disoriented, until I realized what was happening. I looked down to find Adam staring at me with those beautiful blue eyes, now dark with lust and determination.

His mouth was on my cock, warm and insistent. I tried to speak, but I was too sleep-drunk and consumed by lust.

"Adam," I cried.

He didn't stop, even as my hands fisted the sheet and my hips bucked involuntarily. It was too early for my mind to form coherent thoughts, too early to comprehend how this was the same Adam who'd been straight until a few weeks ago.

But, my god, he was good. There was a precision to his movements, a dedication that was all-consuming. A determination to make this good for me. I saw it in his eyes.

"So fucking good, baby. Fuck, Adam, I'm so close."

Without stopping, he smiled and then moaned, applying more suction to the head of my cock. His hand wrapped around my shaft, gripping tight as he stroked and sucked like he'd been doing it forever. Heat spread all over my body. I was ready to combust.

"Adam," I breathed again, his name both a plea and a declaration as I succumbed to the sensations. "I'm gonna—" That was all the warning I could give him as my pleasure crested, and I spilled into his mouth.

When it was over, and the last shudder wracked through my frame, he snaked up my body until we were face-to-face. He crashed his mouth onto mine in a hungry kiss.

"Good morning," he murmured against my lips.

"My turn now."

The morning light had just begun to filter through the sheer curtains, casting a golden hue across Adam's bare skin as I flipped him over.

I ran my hands down his back, marveling at his beautiful curves. He shivered when I placed a kiss between his shoulder blades, his skin filling with tiny goosebumps. He smelled of my soap again, so he must have woken up before me and showered. I was going to take full advantage of that.

"You're going to find out how it feels to be taken by surprise, baby." The first time I used the term of endearment, I'd barely registered it in my lust fog, but when it slipped out again, it felt so right.

Adam moved under my touch, his back undulating as he sought friction from the mattress.

"River…" His voice was a low moan as I parted his cheeks, the sound sending ripples of satisfaction through me.

I lowered my mouth to his hole, and he arched beneath my touch, a gasp escaping him. The taste of him was heady, and I reveled in the way his body responded so viscerally to my touch.

"God, yes," he groaned.

Feeling him unravel, hands fisting the sheet, hips pushing back against me, was the most powerful I'd ever felt. His cock leaked onto the sheet, and I took a moment to appreciate how effortlessly he was coming undone for me.

"River...I'm—" The words were cut off by a sharp intake of breath as his orgasm hit. He came in full-body shudders that seemed to rip through him like a storm. His body jerked until he released a blissful sigh.

I moved up his body, lying beside him and pulling him into my arms. "Now that's how you start your morning," I said, my words tinged with affection and a hint of triumph.

His laugh was breathless. "That was...wow. No wonder both my brothers are with men. I've read about it in romance novels, but why didn't anyone tell me it was *that* good?"

I laughed and placed a kiss on his forehead. "There are certain things you can't experience until you're ready." And I didn't mean just sex but also the connection, the revealing parts of ourselves we hadn't shared with anyone else, and the implicit trust we put in our partner.

"Hey, with the way you loved that, you'd probably enjoy bottoming," I teased.

Adam's laughter was rich and warm. Moments like these reminded me how natural this all felt—how something that could have been fraught with uncertainty instead felt like the most honest expression of who we were together.

Defying my expectations, he surged forward, his lips crashing against mine in a kiss that stole my breath away. "Can we try that...later?"

I blinked, processing the turn of events. "You...want to bottom?"

A tinge of pink colored his chest, neck, and face. "I've been doing some...um...research." He hid his face in the crook of my neck. "I want to be everything you need."

"Fuck, Adam. You already are. You don't need to bottom for me or prove anything." He'd already been every-thing I needed before I got to taste his lips again or find out how beautiful he looked when he gave himself over to an orgasm.

"I know I don't have to, but as evidenced by the pool of cum under me, my body is more than willing to experiment."

"Okay, we'll try later, if you're up for it," I said.

"I'm already up for it." He flipped his leg over mine, showing me how much he really was.

"He's gonna have to wait because we're taking a shower, and then while I make us breakfast, you're going to change the bed sheets. Then we're going out for the best date ever."

"Why do I have to change the bed sheets?" he said with mock indignation.

"Because you made them dirty."

I slapped his ass and jumped out of bed toward the bathroom.

The morning unfolded in a lazy breakfast of pancakes, syrup, and bacon drowned in a gallon of coffee.

"So, what are we doing today that will make it the best date ever?" he asked, scoffing the last of his breakfast.

"David Lima is in Cliffborough for his new cookbook tour," I began, watching as recognition flickered across Adam's features. "He's known for doing couples experiences wherever he goes. I signed us up. Could be fun to learn a new recipe together. What do you think?"

Adam's smile grew wide, his excitement palpable. "You mean *the* David Lima?"

I nodded.

"River, that's…amazing." He sat up, his hand finding mine and squeezing it tightly. "I can't believe you planned this. Mom is going to be so jealous when I tell her."

He got up to clear the plates as I sat dumbfounded. It was the first time he'd mentioned his family in connection to what was happening between us. Would he tell them we were dating?

Was that what we were doing? Fuck. Other than accepting our attraction and connection to each other, we hadn't spoken at all about the outside world.

It wasn't time to panic about something that hadn't happened, so pushing those thoughts aside, I grabbed my plate and cup and took it to the sink where Adam was washing up.

Our afternoon class with David was at a test kitchen downtown. We knocked on the door and were greeted by David himself.

"Welcome," he said. "I'm David. Come on in. I'm so excited for this experience with you guys."

As we stepped into the fully-equipped room, I felt Adam's hand brush against mine. Our eyes met, and we shared a smile. The space was infused with the rich aroma of cocoa and spices like someone had been cooking here since the morning.

"We're really excited, too. I'm River, and this is Adam. Thank you for taking the time to do this with us." I looked around. "Are we the only ones?"

"Yeah, sorry for the change of plans—" David started but was interrupted as a little girl came out of nowhere and crashed into his legs, demanding to be picked up. A tall blond guy followed her, shaking his head.

"Sílvia, sweetheart, what did we agree on?"

The little girl looked at her dad with the biggest blue eyes. "But, Dada. Sílvia cook."

"Sorry, baby," the tall guy said. "I tried, but you know how she is."

David chuckled and then turned to us. "This is Joel, my husband. Our son had to stay home because of school, so she has no one to boss around. Anyway, let's get set up. This little lady will eventually get bored."

"No need to apologize. I'm sure your sous chef has a lot to teach us, right, baby?"

David smiled as I bit my tongue, hoping my slip of the tongue didn't upset Adam. When I looked at him, his face was a cute shade of pink, and he smiled.

We gathered around a table in the middle of the room. There was a bunch of ingredients to one side with a few bowls and mixing spoons next to them.

Joel sat on a stool by the table with Sílvia on his lap.

"Today, we're making Portuguese chocolate salami," David said. His eyes crinkled with amusement as he glanced at Joel. "It's a super easy recipe, but it can get a little messy."

"We like messy," Adam said. "I grew up fighting with my brothers to lick the spoon whenever my mom was baking."

"Today, you don't have to fight anyone to lick the spoon," David said, glancing at his husband, whose face turned the same shade of pink as Adam's.

The recipe was simple enough. We started by mixing sugar and eggs in a bowl. David said we wanted to dissolve the sugar as much as possible before adding the chocolate powder.

I didn't miss the knowing smiles David and Joel shared as we followed the recipe

It was obvious how much they loved each other. Were Adam and I as obvious? Could people tell by the way Adam's laughter seemed to caress me or that our gazes always lingered a beat too long?

"Okay, this is when it starts to get messy," David instructed, guiding us through the steps to add the melted chocolate and butter.

"I have a confession to make," Adam said. "My mom has made hundreds of these, but I've only ever engaged in the licking part."

I snorted, and Adam elbowed me.

"How does this get to be a salami shape?" I asked.

"Do you have Portuguese or Italian heritage?" David asked Adam.

"Mom's family is Portuguese. Dad's is American."

"Just like mine," Joel said as he straightened the little ponytail on his daughter's hair.

"Oh really? I didn't know that."

"Yeah, in fact, we were going to check out a Portuguese restaurant for an early dinner. That is if we can get a table without booking. Have you heard of Lusitana? We've heard amazing things about their food. Would you like to join us?" Joel asked.

Adam and I exchanged a quick glance. He smiled, so I knew he'd be on board with what I was about to suggest.

"Actually, I'm the manager of Lusitana. Adam's parents own it. I'm sure you can score a place at the chef's table." I winked and said, "I'll just need to make a call as soon as my fingers aren't covered in chocolate."

Adam took my hand and brought it up to his mouth, licking off every bit of chocolate. My cock hardened as my mind took me to this morning's events.

"Adam." I tried to sound indignant, but it came out all croaky.

"Now you can make the call." He shrugged.

My chin practically hit the floor. I couldn't even look at David and Joel. All of a sudden, they started laughing.

"Score us that table, and over dinner, we'll tell you how David went viral with his chocolate salami class on social media." Joel bit his lip as David managed to visibly blush, even with his tan skin.

I took my phone out and called Fir to set a table for four in the kitchen. It was something we did for special guests on occasion.

"Okay, back to the class," David said.

He taught us how to roll the cookie-and-chocolate mix into a sausage shape using two sheets of grease-proof paper.

"Looks perfect," David proclaimed. "It needs to set in the fridge for a few hours, ideally overnight. We have a gift for you." He presented us with a custom cool box, its sides adorned with intricate patterns reminiscent of Portuguese tiles. "For your chocolate salami, to enjoy later."

"Thank you," I said. "This is very generous."

"The pleasure is all mine. There are a lot of things I don't get to do anymore. Between book tours and cooking shows, I miss connecting with people. I started off in my mom's café. She taught me everything I know. One of my favorite things is cooking for other people," David said.

"River," Adam said softly, once David and Joel were preoccupied with their daughter, who'd fallen asleep in her dad's arms. "Thank you for this. It's been so much fun."

"And now I know how you learned to lick and suck so well," I teased.

He grabbed my hand and whispered intently, "Remember what you promised earlier."

26

ADAM

WE STUMBLED into River's place, our lips locked in a desperate dance of tongues and warm breath. My hands roamed his body with a need I couldn't recall ever possessing, greedily pulling him closer. Each caress from him ignited a fire that had been smoldering since this morning when he'd worshipped my ass like it was the best meal he'd ever had.

"Adam," he murmured between kisses. His hands were just as eager, exploring my back and slipping beneath my shirt to trace the skin he found there.

All day, I'd thought about the way he'd rimmed me, the way my body sang with pleasure, and the anticipation from his promise to let me bottom for him.

We left a trail of discarded clothes on our way to the bedroom.

"River," I gasped when we finally broke apart for air, my voice raspy with desire. "I haven't stopped thinking about, about…you know."

"I need words, Adam."

"And I need you to fuck me, River." There, I said it.

His eyes, framed by dark lashes, met mine. "Are you sure?" His voice was soft yet firm.

"More than anything," I whispered, and it was true. I'd done my research. I knew it would hurt, and that scared me, mostly because I was afraid that, in the end, I wouldn't be able to do it. At the same time, I knew nothing had ever felt more right than being with River, surrendering to the pull I suspected had always existed between us but I'd been blind to.

"Get on the bed and hold your legs up to your chest," he commanded.

I practically jumped on it, my hard cock slapping against my heated skin. "Fuck, that's so hot."

My heart hammered as he lowered himself to me, going straight for the kill. I cried in pleasure when he ran his tongue from my hole all the way up to the head of my cock. When he sucked it to the back of his throat, I almost jumped off the bed.

"River!" I cried.

"You taste so fucking good, baby."

"Nghnn, you have to stop that, or I'll come before we have a chance to get things going."

He chuckled as he kissed my hole, pulling back with a soft blow that failed to cool my heated skin. "Oh, things are definitely going."

My body felt like it was on the verge of something world-changing, but I could feel his hesitance in the way his fingers traced patterns on my skin.

"Adam," he said. "I think we should wait."

I stilled at his words.

No. Waiting was not an option. Not when every fiber of my being was alight with the need to be with him like this.

"River," I breathed out, my resolve hardening as I pulled

him closer so we could be face-to-face. "I can't wait. I've never been so sure about anything."

The truth was, I craved the intimacy, the connection from having him fill me. I couldn't explain it, but I needed to find out how that felt.

He studied me, his eyes searching for a gap in my resolve. "I have a proposition for you."

"Go on…"

"Top me first. If neither of us comes, then…then, I'll top you."

I saw the challenge in his eyes. Daring me to a game of patience and control. It didn't matter how it ended because every outcome was a win for me.

"All right," I agreed, though every inch of me screamed to be claimed by him instead. "You know how competitive I can be. You're on."

He kissed me gently. "I do know how competitive you can be. It's one of the things I find so appealing about you. You don't give up even when all evidence points otherwise."

"So, I'm basically stubborn."

"If the hat fits."

My hands roamed his back, mapping every curve and dip of muscle until I was able to grope his ass and separate his cheeks. I ran my finger down his crease until I felt the puckered skin of his hole. "I'm going to own this tonight."

"Adam," he breathed out, his voice threaded with that same need that pulsed through my veins.

He closed his eyes when I pressed my finger as though I were trying to get inside him. I wouldn't without lube, but watching his lips tremble with the need for more, I was suddenly all on board with the new plan.

I flipped us over until he was the one on his back. I went down on his cock, savoring the saltiness of his skin. The unique flavor that was unmistakably River. His cock was hard against my tongue, leaking precum that I lapped up greedily. Who knew cock could taste so good?

But then, amid the haze of arousal, a practical thought flickered to life. "Condoms. Do you have any?"

"In the bedside table. Lube too." His voice was thick with arousal, now laced with impatience.

I pulled away just enough to fish out the needed items, the packet crinkling in my eager hands. He watched me, eyes darkened with want and something deeper, something that made my heart stutter.

Lubricant in hand, I squeezed some on my fingers, circling his entrance before pushing one inside. He squirmed, soft moans escaping his lips. "Adam," he breathed out, each syllable laced with pleasure.

"God, River," I breathed, my own arousal spiraling out of control.

When he started moving against my finger, I added a second.

"Curl your fingers up like this," he said, showing me what he meant. As soon as I did it, he almost jumped off the bed like he'd been electrocuted.

"What happened? Did I hurt you?" I asked, pulling out.

"Fuck no. Please do that again. With three fingers."

I did, and River's reaction was the same. Every time my fingers brushed over the spongy button inside, he completely lost it.

"Fuck, that's your prostate, isn't it?"

He nodded, biting his lower lip, his breath coming in short bursts. "I'm ready. Fuck, I'm so ready, baby."

"Are you sure?"

He nodded, and with a trembling hand, I suited up and aligned with his body. The push into him was slow, deliberate, forcing me to take in every shred of sensation—the scorching heat, the velvety tightness. It was unlike anything I had ever felt, this overwhelming sense of rightness as I became part of him in the most intimate way.

"Adam…" he whispered, his voice cracking on my name. As I began to move, I realized this wasn't just physical. Every thrust into him was the culmination of every unspoken word, every shared glance was the beginning of something irreversible, and I never wanted it to end.

We fell into a rhythm punctuated by the sound of skin slapping against skin while the rest of the world faded away.

"Adam," he gasped, his voice hitching as I hit that perfect spot inside him, "it's…incredible."

"I feel it too, River. Fuck, I feel it." All those years of friendship were funneling into this singular moment, transforming into something deeper, something fierce and unbreakable.

Fuck. I wanted to feel him inside me too.

I wanted to know how it felt to have River move inside me, his strong body over mine, claiming me. But as I watched his expression flicker between delight and sheer bliss, I realized that before I got there, I needed to give this to him.

I adjusted my angle, seeking that perfect depth, as River threw his head back. He held on to my arms, and my eyes narrowed on his beautiful tattoo of the coffee molecule peeking out from under his left arm. Chemistry. It seemed oddly fitting because we had plenty of it.

"Keep going," he urged, his legs tightening around me.

And I did. I lost myself in the push and pull, the heat, the friction, and the mounting pressure at the base of my spine. Soon, my moans matched his, echoing off the walls of his bedroom.

"River, I'm—" I couldn't even finish the sentence. The world narrowed to the explosive sensation ripping through me, drawing out my orgasm. It hit me like a tidal wave, intense and all-consuming. His body tensed beneath me as he followed suit.

We were panting, sweating, our hearts beating wildly out of sync yet somehow perfectly aligned. Collapsing beside him, I reached for his hand, intertwining our fingers.

"Thank you," I whispered as I kissed every knuckle on his hand. "that was more than perfect." I wanted to say more, but the only words I had for how I felt were way too big.

Whether as friends or lovers, we'd crossed a threshold tonight.

"You have no idea how perfect it was for me, baby," he whispered, his voice stuck in his throat, and there it was, that endearment that made my heart sing every time he called me that.

He'd orchestrated the perfect date. We'd laughed with new friends, bonding over our shared Portuguese heritage, which River had experienced first-hand with my family.

It'd been thoughtful, so damn thoughtful, in the way only River could manage.

"Today was amazing," I said as I got rid of the condom and stepped into the bathroom to grab a towel to clean the mess we made. No way I was changing the sheets again.

"Because it was with you," he replied when I lay beside him. He wrapped his arms around me tight, like he never wanted to let me go.

"This scares me, you know?" I confessed.

"It scares me too, Adam. More than you know."

"Are you awake?" Adam whispered against my chest.

"I am now."

"Sorry, I didn't mean to—"

I cradled his face and tilted it up. I couldn't see him in the dark, but I didn't need light to know the expression he was wearing. His voice told me everything.

"Hey, baby. What's in your head?"

He sighed.

"You."

I chuckled.

"Thinking about me is keeping you awake? Maybe I didn't do a good enough job a few hours ago." I tugged him closer and closed my lips over his. He responded immediately, opening for me and giving me a taste of his sweet mouth.

"Why is it so good with you?" he asked, his voice filled with wonder. "I don't understand it. I've been trying to figure out what I am, but…"

"Can I turn the light on?" I asked.

I felt Adam nod, so I stretched over to the table on my side and turned on the light.

"There you are," I said, pulling him back against me.

He rested his chin on my chest, his eyes firmly on mine. "Was it hard for you to come out?"

"No. I always knew my mom would love me no matter what, and I always felt safe with your family. Noah had already come out by the time I came out, so it was easy."

"How about the demisexual part? You never told me about that."

I knew that question would come eventually. It was a fair one. Why would I have kept something like that from my best friend? The answer was that I wouldn't. Not unless my best friend had been the reason I'd figured that part of myself out.

"I'm sorry. I didn't mean to keep it from you. I guess…it didn't seem like it was that important. I'm still gay, and I'm still me."

He bit his lip and let out a contemplative sigh.

"Does it bother you that I didn't say anything?" I asked.

He traced a pattern on my chest with his finger. "No. I mean, I think it did at first, but then when I started feeling differently about you, I got it. Your sexuality is yours, and you don't owe me or anyone else full disclosure."

"Thank you." I laced our fingers together, bringing his hand to my lips and kissing his warm skin. "What's really on your mind?"

"I don't know who I am. Am I gay? Bi? Pansexual? I considered that maybe I'm demisexual like you because this thing, this connection I have with you…I don't think I could have it with another man. But then again, I don't think I could have it with anyone, which just shreds to pieces everything I knew about myself and the fact I was about to marry Victoria and—"

"Hey," I interrupted gently, running my free hand over his back. "Sexuality is fluid. You know that, right?"

He nodded, so I continued, "First, you don't have to figure it all out in one go, and you also don't need to label yourself. If you feel better without a label, that's okay. If you need to define yourself with a label, that's okay too. You can take your time figuring out what that label is."

"I guess. I wish it were easier."

"It can be, baby. Are you happy here with me?"

Adam looked up, and his smile reached the depths of my heart. It wrapped around it and made it miss a few beats. "More than I ever could have imagined. I never thought I'd ever be naked in a bed with you and feel like I want to get so close to you that I'm inside your skin."

I chuckled. "I'm a little concerned now."

He hooked his leg over mine, and before I had the chance to react, he was on top of me.

"What concerns you? That you and your body seem to make my dick hard now?" he asked, moving against me and making *my* dick hard. "Or is it that you find me so irresistible?"

I groaned. "You're irresistible, all right. And a demon. I have work tomorrow, you know that?"

"Hmm, but it's still today, so we're still technically on our date."

I'd argue that three in the morning is very much the next day, but why would I when my whole body was fine-tuned to Adam and had very little desire to sleep?

"I suppose you have a point."

After that, I shut down my brain and our conversation to focus solely on making sure we both got off again. Sleep be damned.

The loud noise of elephant footsteps outside the room shattered the early morning stillness, dragging me from a dreamless sleep. My heart jolted as I blinked into consciousness. Adam's breath was a steady rhythm against my neck. His body was curled into mine in a way that was now so familiar. Who'd have known he was a cuddler?

As the racket grew louder, my brain woke the rest up.

Fuck. They're here.

Adam, still fast asleep, remained oblivious to the impending chaos his brothers were about to unleash upon us. I hesitated for a moment, caught between the desire to wake him gently and the necessity of urgency. But time was a luxury we didn't have. In fact, it was slipping away with each heavy footfall on the wooden floor.

"Fuck," I muttered under my breath, a mix of fear, anticipation, and the dawning that our secret was about to come out.

Adam stirred beside me, a soft sigh escaping him as if he also sensed the turning point we teetered upon. His eyes opened slowly, and he smiled.

"River?" The word was thick with sleep, his voice a groggy babble that normally would've made me smile. "What's that noise?"

I wanted nothing more than to press my lips against his in a quiet good morning, to savor the softness of his mouth and the way he'd melt against me. But the thunderous approach of his brothers denied us even that simple pleasure.

"Adam! River! Wake the fuck up."

"What the—"

"They're here," I breathed out.

I sat up abruptly, pulling the duvet over Adam's body in a fluid motion. The door slammed open just as I managed to arrange the covers into a semblance of innocent disarray.

Noah loomed in the doorway, "Where's Adam? Did you

know he's not in his room?" His question was less inquiry and more accusation.

"Maybe he's out for an early run," I said, my voice steady despite the pounding in my heart. It was a plausible lie. I hadn't seen Adam run unless he was being chased, but it could happen, right?

Lex stepped in behind Noah. "Where's Adam?"

I met Lex's gaze. He was the one I couldn't lie to. Not completely, because he'd see right through me.

"Adam's around," I said carefully. "Just…tied up at the moment."

Beneath the covers, Adam lay still.

Emery followed behind, his steps halting as he saw me, as though he hadn't expected me to be in my own bed. His dark eyes flickered to the bed, a quick, piercing glance that took in the shape beneath the duvet. His lips quirked, not quite a smile, not quite a frown, but he said nothing, only arched an eyebrow.

"Looks like you're a man down," I commented, trying to keep my voice light.

"Lior is in the living room," Noah said, his eyes scanning the discarded clothes all over my bedroom floor. "He doesn't want any part in this."

"Part in what?" I asked, feigning ignorance while my pulse thrummed against my throat. Adam remained motionless beneath the duvet, the stillness of his form almost convincing.

"Our home invasion." He rolled his eyes. "He's still a little traumatized from when you all did this to us. Anyway. Why do you have so many pillows under your blankets?" The question hung between us. I had to get rid of them because it was only a matter of time until they found out.

"Uh, bad back," I lied smoothly, or at least I hoped it was smooth.

"Since when?" Emery finally chimed in, his voice soft but laced with a knowing undertone. He was too observant for his own good—or mine.

"Since…recently. Um…carrying boxes at the restaurant."

"Bad back, huh?" Lex said, still oblivious to his twin's burning presence against my legs. "You should let Adam give you a massage. I hear he's got magic hands."

"Maybe later," I replied, trying to sound casual.

Adam chuckled beside me, so I coughed loudly and kneed him to keep quiet.

"Anyway," Noah said. "Adam's not here, so we can ask you. We want to know how you and Adam managed to have dinner with David Lima and his husband last night at Lusitana."

"*That* is the reason you're invading my place?" I asked, relaxing slightly and hoping that answering their questions would get them to move along soon.

Noah looked at Lex and Emery and then back at me. "Why else would we invade your sacred"—he glanced at the clothes on the floor—"and extremely messy sanctuary?"

"You need to check out the definition of sanctuary," I said.

"Bish, bosh. Fess up, Hartley," Lex said.

"Adam and I attended one of David's experiences. As it turned out, they'd been hoping to get a table at Lusitana, so I invited them to dine with us. That's all."

"Aren't those experiences for couples only?" Emery asked.

The question hung there, dangling like a carrot, waiting for me to bite.

"Is he as gorgeous in real life?" Lex asked

"David Lima?" I echoed, grasping the change of subject like a lifeline. "He's…striking, sure. But you know, he's a genuinely nice guy. His husband too."

"I wish I'd been there," Lex sighed.

"How do you even know about it?" I asked.

"Drew," Noah replied before his eyes stilled on the form next to me. "Why are your pillows breathing?" Noah asked.

"Breathing?" I feigned puzzled amusement.

"Yeah, breathing…" His voice trailed off as Lior's shout echoed from the living room.

"You're all seriously dumb if you still haven't figured out what's happening here. River, I'm going to make myself a coffee."

Noah's lips parted, then closed. If he frowned any more, he'd need to consider Botox.

Lex gasped as he seemed to finally realize what was happening.

"Make that three coffees, Lior!" I called out, a touch more loudly than necessary. Laughter bubbled from below the duvet.

28

———

ADAM

"Lior is right. How do you all not get what's going on here?" My brothers' shocked expressions met me as I sat up, pulling the sheet flush with my body.

I already felt bare coming from under the covers. There was no need to be completely naked too.

I looked at River, his eyes meeting mine, a silent question lingering in his gaze. I wanted nothing more than to melt back into the warmth of his arms, to forget the world beyond this bed, but I couldn't ignore my brothers and Emery's presence.

"Could have told you if you'd asked," Lior's voice sliced through the stillness from the living room. His I-told-you-so tone almost made me laugh.

"Baby, we're going to have a serious conversation when we get home," Noah shouted back.

Lex's expression was a contorted puzzle of confusion and curiosity as he stood there, his gaze flitting between River and me. "What's all this? Just a sleepover gone…wild?" He gestured vaguely toward the tangled bedding and our bare skin.

"Lex, have you ever had naked sleepovers with your best friends?" I asked, locking eyes with him.

He shifted uncomfortably, the corners of his mouth twitching. "Well, Emery's my best friend, so…sort of, yeah."

"Case in point," I said, rolling my eyes. "This is what we're doing."

River put his arms around my waist, anchoring me. After the conversation we'd had last night, I knew he'd be understandably concerned, but I was tired of hiding.

If I couldn't be myself with my brothers, who could I be honest with?

"Told you so," Noah said, turning to Lex.

"You did not."

"You said you saw them kissing when you were fourteen. How are you surprised by this?"

"You saw it?" I asked in shock. "Why didn't you say anything?"

Lex shrugged. "I figured you'd tell me eventually, and when you didn't, I thought it was just an experimentation that didn't mean anything." He chuckled. "We all experimented, right?"

"Some more than others," Noah, the resident sexual prodigy, said.

I turned to River. "I'm sorry our first kiss…wasn't our first kiss…"

River brought his hand up to my face and ran his thumb over my cheek. My eyes fluttered closed before I opened them again to gaze into his green depths. "No, baby. Our first kiss was *my* first kiss. Your first kiss with me was definitely not that kiss when we were fourteen."

"How does that work?" I chuckled.

"You know that feeling you got when we kissed? I got that all those years ago. It's just that you took a little longer to catch up. It's okay. Your skill has improved a lot since then."

"Oh yeah?" I smiled, my gaze moving back to his soft lips and the short beard that framed his face perfectly.

A cough reminded me we weren't alone.

Crap.

"Hey," I whispered. "How legal is it to kill your siblings?"

"Not legal at all."

I turned back to my brothers and Emery.

"Any chance you guys can fuck off so we can get dressed?"

The three of them crossed their arms and stayed put.

"What will it take for you fuckers to get out of the room?" I asked in exasperation before they started making kissy noises.

I turned to River, who winked at me before pressing his mouth against mine in the dirtiest kiss to top all dirty kisses.

My brain fully stopped when all my blood rushed to my cock.

I didn't know at what point they all left the room, but I hoped it was before I straddled River, taking the covers with me.

"Hmm, fuck, baby, I only wanted to give them a taste of their own medicine, not a show," he said into my lips as I chased his for another kiss.

"Then you shouldn't have kissed me like that. You know your mouth makes me stupid."

He chuckled. "It's not on purpose."

"Sure, it isn't." I kissed down his jaw and his neck, sucking a patch of warm skin. "So, fourteen…"

"Huh?"

I pulled back to look at him. "You really liked that kiss when we were fourteen."

"It's lived rent-free in my head ever since, although it has recently been replaced by other life events."

"Like me entering your body and claiming you?"

He placed his hands on my ass, pulling me closer and grinding our cocks together.

"I take that as a yes," I said, freeing the covers trapped between us. I moaned when I finally felt skin on skin. "Fuck, River. Feels so good."

"Your door is still open. We can hear everything!" Noah shouted.

"Then you have a choice: leave or cover your ears," I shouted back before turning to River. "Do you think if we're really loud, they'll leave for good?"

His laughter was a rich sound. "I have to work today, remember? But to be fair, we deserve the payback."

I pouted as I glanced at our still-hard cocks pressed together. "Sorry, guys. Not my fault."

River laughed, but then he caressed my face gently. "Are you okay? As coming outs go, this was quite a spectacular one." His question was gentle, eyes searching mine for signs of panic.

"Yeah, I think I am." The reality of what lay ahead was daunting. The conversation that awaited outside the sanctuary of River's room was filled with explanations and admissions, but I knew my brothers loved me no matter what. They'd understand, maybe more than anyone apart from River, what I was going through.

We dressed in silence, an easy routine we'd become used to. When I pulled one of his T-shirts from his drawer, I realized I'd been doing that a lot lately.

When he'd run out of clean ones, he'd gone to the other bedroom and brought mine over to his drawer, so they were all mixed now.

I stopped in motion, my brain taking me back to when

I'd moved in with Victoria. There had been a clear delineation of which spaces were hers and which were mine.

River buttoned his work shirt, rolling up the sleeves until I was able to catch a glimpse of his tattoos. He caught me staring but said nothing. Just sent me a brief smile that said more than any words he may have shared.

"Time to face the music," I said, turning to the bedroom door.

If I had expected the air to be heavy with anticipation or my brother's curious gazes to follow our every move as we entered the living room, I'd have been wrong.

"We made you coffee," Lex said, pointing at the two mugs on the coffee table.

"Pancakes are coming right up," Emery shouted from the kitchen. "Sorry, I was hungry."

River's hand found mine, a silent show of support…that I didn't think I needed because it looked like the shock of finding us in the same bed had worn off and they were being their usual selves.

"Good morning, Lior," I said.

"Morning," he replied with his coffee cup in hand while Noah sat crossways on his lap. "Once again, my apologies for this morning."

I smiled. "I think it's safe to say we deserved it."

"Damn right," Lex said. "I need to take Emery home after this to detraumatize my eyes."

"You don't have ice cream," Emery said accusatorily, coming in from the kitchen with a stack of plates in one hand and a plate with a huge stack of pancakes in the other.

"That's okay, baby. We have all the ice cream at home," Lex said, holding his hand out to Emery, who took it after putting the load he was carrying on the table.

"So," Noah started. "Are you guys dating?"

"We've had two dates, so yeah, I guess," I said.

"I don't think we can count painting rooms as a date," River said.

"Sure we can. First, I took you out for breakfast, and then we kissed."

We exchanged a look and smiled.

"Fuck me, this is serious," Noah said.

I stared at him. "What do you mean?"

He shrugged. "Look, I can't profess to say I know what it's like to be a late bloomer because we all know I so wasn't."

Lior snorted.

Noah hit his chest lightly before continuing, "But you guys have always been super close. Like more than best friends are. It was only a matter of time until all the parts of your body caught up. And for once, I don't mean your dick."

"I really didn't know, you know?" I said, and they all gave me understanding smiles. "It was like one day we were friends, and the next, I was checking out his ass and having all these other thoughts."

"Aww, baby, you're so romantic," River joked.

"Wait up, when did it happen? Because…you know…the wedding," Lex said.

My hand paused on the way to adding a couple of pancakes to my plate.

Even though my non-wedding day turned out to be a blessing, I still couldn't shake off everything that had happened. Having to tell everyone I knew, and then the radio silence from Victoria. It was still a sore point.

"The honeymoon," I muttered.

Lex gasped. "So, all the jokes we made…"

I shook my head. "Nothing happened for a few weeks. That was just when I started paying attention."

"Anyway," River said, changing the subject. "What did you come here for? I know it wasn't to catch us in bed, and it can't be all about our dinner with David Lima and his husband."

"We pulled some strings, so Drew and West's fundraiser auction is in two weeks. We have a lot of work to do, so we're skipping Sunday lunch and going to the office. We'll get takeout later. We were coming to pick you up."

I laughed. "All those things could have been conveyed via text."

"Yeah, but we wanted to ask you about David Lima."

We shared all the gossip until River had to go to work and I had to leave with my brothers, Emery, and Lior to go to the office where West would meet us since Drew was also working.

"See you later, boyfriend," I said, tasting the word in my mouth, and fuck if it didn't feel right.

River stared at me in shock. "Adam…"

"It doesn't have to be that now, River, but I'd like it to be at some point."

He pulled me into his arms and kissed me hard. "See you later, boyfriend."

The catcalls from my brothers as we kissed were totally unnecessary, but I wouldn't deny it felt good to have approval from the people who mattered the most to me.

It felt damn good. Now, all I needed was to convince them to not put me up for auction at the fundraiser because there was no way I wanted to give up any of my future free time to anyone who wasn't River.

29

RIVER

I ADJUSTED the platters of hors d'oeuvres, more to keep busy than the need to ensure each display was perfect. They already were, thanks to my team. While Fir and the chef kept Lusitana open tonight, the sous chef and a team of agency servers were with me at the Star Finders Foundation Charity Auction and Gala.

With a final check, I felt a hand slip into mine. The noise of the guests entering the venue became a distant hum as Adam guided me away from the bustle, his fingers interlocking with mine.

We slipped through a side door into the tree peony collection.

Adam didn't hesitate. His lips claimed mine with a passion that stole my breath. "I missed you," he said when he pulled away.

I searched his face, the blue of his eyes darkening. Did he miss me amid the chaos of the preparation for the event, or was it more? We were still together every night, even if, in the last two weeks, I'd barely taken my fill of him in a few stolen moments before sleep took us away.

"I don't want to be auctioned off," he said, pouting.

"Come on," I laughed, "you're not selling your body, just lending your mind for a good cause."

"I know, but it means having to schedule time with someone else. That's less time with you."

"Baby," I began, my tone softening as I reached out to touch his arm. My thumb brushed over the fabric of his sleeve. "We live together, remember? You're in my space every day and night."

His pout grew bigger, if that was possible, so I leaned over and sucked his lower lip into my mouth, humming my appreciation of his soft lips and sweet taste.

"Have you been happy there?" I asked. "At my place, I mean. Or have you thought about finding somewhere else to live?"

Why was I bringing this up now? I hated that my insecurities and my fear of losing Adam now that I had him took over, but it had been weeks since Lex and Noah found out about us, and he still hadn't told his parents.

"In case it hasn't been clear from the way I search for you even in my sleep, I am very happy living with you." His brows narrowed. "Unless…do you want me to move out? Are we doing this wrong? Is it too fast?"

I put a finger over his mouth. "Hey, I love having you with me, and I'm definitely not suggesting you move anywhere. It's just a little hard for me to work with your parents and feel like I'm lying to them whenever they ask about you."

He opened his mouth to talk, but I kept my finger in place. "You need to take your time deciding how and when you want to tell them. I'm just expressing my feelings because I care about you so much, Adam. I want us to be able to communicate."

"River," he whispered, and the way he said my name felt like a caress and an apology.

"Tonight," I whispered against the warmth of his lips, "when all this is over, it'll be just us, and we'll make up for the time lost over the last two weeks."

"I'm holding you to that," Adam murmured, his voice husky.

Reluctantly, I pulled away, my fingers tracing the line of his jaw before dropping to my side.

"Come on, I have work to do, and you need to go out there and be charming."

"Fine." He sulked but then straightened and gave me his most charming smile.

I'd pay a million dollars for it every day, but knowing he gave it freely whenever our eyes met was an instant rush to my heart.

I'm in so much fucking trouble.

Outside our hideout, the event buzzed with anticipation. While Adam left me to meet up with West and Drew, I moved through the crowd, seeking familiar faces among the staff. They were a well-trained team, but without Fir at my side, I felt the extra responsibility on my shoulders.

"Jenna, remember to smile and offer the canapés with both hands," I instructed one of the agency servers. Her nod was earnest, her eyes bright.

"Mark, pace yourself with the wine pours—generous, but not too generous," I reminded another, who gave me a knowing wink.

As the auction drew near, I took one final look around. The botanical gardens had been transformed into an elegant backdrop for the evening.

I took my place at the side of the room, with a full view of the kitchen door and the servers as they moved around each other like a choreographed dance.

The crowd hushed as the emcee took the stage, his voice rich and inviting.

Adam was first on the list, which both thrilled and terrified me. Despite my earlier reassurance, the reality of watching others bid on his time gnawed at me with sharp teeth.

"Let's start the bidding for Mr. Adam Spencer," the emcee announced, his words laced with enthusiasm. "A wordsmith whose skills are only matched by his compassion and philanthropism. The winning bidder will not only enjoy his company but also have access to one of the great marketing and PR minds of this city."

I watched Adam, standing tall and poised, a light flush on his cheeks betraying the calm he projected. His eyes met mine for an instant, a silent plea for reassurance. I nodded subtly, my support unwavering, yet my stomach twisted into knots.

"Five hundred dollars!" called out a voice, igniting the first spark of the bidding war.

"Seven hundred!" another countered swiftly.

"Adam Spencer, folks, an entrepreneur who started a PR company with his brothers fresh out of college, determined to build up new businesses in our community," the emcee continued.

"Two thousand!" a new bid echoed, more assertive.

"Three thousand five hundred!" The numbers grew, and with each raise, I was prouder and prouder that my man's talent with words was being recognized by so many.

"Can we hear four?" the emcee goaded, his smile predatory.

"Ten thousand!" The room gasped collectively, followed by a wave of chattering.

"Fifty-five thousand!" The voice cut through the air like a knife, silencing the murmurs around the room.

"Seven hundred and fifty more!" It was the same voice, making the total an unusual fifty-five thousand seven hundred and fifty dollars. What a random number.

My pulse hammered in my ears, the sound drowning out the final gavel as the emcee declared, "Sold!"

My gaze darted across the sea of faces, landing on the figure behind the voice.

I would have recognized the profile even from a distance, even if I hadn't connected the voice to it immediately.

Victoria stood poised at the edge of the gathered crowd, a sly triumph etched into the refined angles of her face. Her gaze locked on Adam's.

His Adam's apple bobbed as he stood frozen on the stage. The emcee sang praises to Adam's ability to command such a high bid and how the money raised would help the disadvantaged children of Cliffborough as well as their families.

Victoria bent her knees to pick up the train of her perfectly fitted dress. Her hair was styled to one side, and there was not a single flaw in her porcelain complexion.

She sauntered around the wide columns on the periphery of the room. Her eyes remained on Adam, but she slowed to a stop in front of me and smiled.

"Quite the generous donation," I remarked, hoping to keep any kind of emotion from my voice.

"Adam's worth every penny," she responded.

Anger bubbled inside me.

Worth every penny?

Was he worth every penny when she put the note under my door on their wedding day? Was he worth every penny when he had to stand on a fucking chair to tell both their families she'd left him?

My eyes darted across the room to Adam's brothers. Noah's stare alone gave me the strength to keep my composure.

The moment stretched between us. If she was baiting me into a reaction, she was shit out of luck.

"Looks like you've got some planning to do," I observed, my voice betraying none of my internal rage. Or the desire to claim Adam openly.

"It seems so," she replied, resuming her measured walk toward Adam.

I fisted my hands beside me when she kissed Adam on the cheek.

"River?"

It turned to one of the servers. "Yeah?"

"We ran out of the smoked salmon hors d'oeuvres."

"Check the cafeteria kitchen. We're using their fridge for extras since they're closed. If we've really run out, pick something else."

When I turned back toward Adam and Victoria, all I saw was the red of her dress as she left through a side door.

I scanned the room, looking for Adam, but I couldn't find him.

"Aren't you going after them?" Noah asked, appearing out of nowhere.

"I..." I was as frozen in my spot as Adam had been on stage earlier.

"You have to go," Emery said.

"What if they—"

"No." Noah cut me off. "This is not the time to go back to the sidelines. We've watched you do that all your life. Adam belongs with you, not that broomstick-less witch."

"Please, River," Lex pleaded.

It's not that I didn't want to go, but between seeing the pain in Adam's eyes when he saw Victoria and witnessing her overbearing display of confidence, I'd lost all of mine.

Noah shook me. "Either you go or I will, and we both know that won't end well."

"And you think it'll end better if I go in?" I laughed.

"Yeah, you won't commit actual murder."

I stared at the door they'd walked through and then remembered the fear and sadness in Adam's eyes. My feet moved before my brain caught up.

30

———

ADAM

ONCE I GOT past the shock that held me hostage while I was on stage with hundreds of eyes on me, it was a different emotion that got me moving.

Rage.

How dare Victoria show up now, today of all days, and place *that* bid. The number meant nothing to everyone in the audience, but for me, it was the final twist of the knife in my back.

I'd hesitated for a fraction of a second, watching Victoria detach herself from the crowd. The way she moved, with choreographed grace and every step measured, was achingly familiar.

With a deep breath that did little to ease the tightness in my chest, I'd followed her. I'd taken a quick glance at River but couldn't keep my eyes on him because if he'd met mine, it would have been too tempting to ask for his support.

He'd been there for me when I needed him the most, and now he was more important to me than ever, which was why I needed to do this on my own. If nothing else, I'd prove to myself that I was truly over Victoria.

Besides, this was between Victoria and me.

As the door closed behind us, the murmur of guests and clinking glasses fell into a hush. The safety of River and my brothers' support was on the other side of the heavy door.

I stopped by a cluster of blooms. The roses, so beautiful and delicate with their calming scent, could also draw blood with their thorns. That was Victoria. And in *that* dress. The one she'd spent months telling me about until I bought it for her. The one she'd planned on wearing the evening of our wedding day. She looked…deadly.

She was as much a thorny rose as the displays around us.

Looking into her eyes, I searched for the woman I thought I knew, but in that moment, standing before her, it struck me. We were strangers, with nothing but memories to suggest we'd once been more.

"Victoria," I said, surprised at how steady my voice sounded.

"Adam," she replied, her voice soft, confident and poised.

"Why are you here?"

She glanced around the rose exhibition. "We had our engagement party here. It was a beautiful evening."

Yeah, one that had triggered my twin brother because this was where he'd chosen to propose to Emery before he disappeared. At the time, I'd believed Victoria hadn't meant to hurt Lex and simply wanted to have our party in a beautiful setting.

The thought that I'd trusted her so much that I'd believed everything she said, only for her to do what she did to me and my family, made me sick to my stomach.

"I'm not here to reminisce. What do you want, Victoria?

"

"I want to talk," she said finally, her gaze settling back on me.

"Talk?" I laughed. "And you chose now? In the middle of

a public setting? A charity event?" I couldn't keep the incredulity from seeping into my tone. "Couldn't you have called me? Set up a meeting somewhere…private?"

She tucked a non-existent stray lock of hair behind her ear. "Would you have answered, Adam?"

I exhaled, a slow release of the tension that had built since I'd had to stand on top of a chair to tell our families she was gone. She knew me well enough to know the answer.

"Exactly," she whispered.

"Where have you been, Victoria?" My voice found its footing, firmer this time, laced with a quiet demand for long-overdue answers.

"I've been away," she said at last. "Thinking about life… about some of the things I did. The decisions we sometimes make that can affect other people's lives."

The air between us became charged, every unspoken accusation crackling in the silence. I folded my arms across my chest. "Like abandoning the man you supposedly loved on your wedding day," I said, the words falling like lead between us, "and leaving him to deal with the fallout."

Victoria's eyes, once warm and familiar, now held a cool distance. "I've transferred the money for the wedding expenses to your account," she announced, her voice steadier than I expected. The revelation should have brought some sense of justice, a settling of scores, but instead, it felt hollow. "And I've matched that with a donation to Star Finders," she continued. Was this some hollow attempt at atonement? "I know it won't absolve me of what I did, but it's a start to making things right."

A multitude of responses built on the tip of my tongue: anger, sarcasm, maybe even gratitude for the gesture, but they all fell away, unsaid.

The stillness of the room was broken by the soft tread of approaching footsteps.

River's sudden presence eased the tension brought on by Victoria.

"Adam?" His voice held a note of concern. He stood there, his eyes searching mine, a silent question hovering between us. "Are you okay?"

The words were simple, but they carried the weight of our years of friendship, every shared secret, every quiet moment of understanding. Only weeks ago, that question had become a stone in my shoe. Everyone wanted to know how Adam Spencer was coping with the tragedy of being jilted on his wedding day.

I'd grown to hate the question because there was only one acceptable and expected answer. I managed a smile. "I'm fine, River," I assured him, though "fine" felt like a foreign concept.

River's gaze didn't waver. He knew me too well.

I wanted to reach out to him, take his hand, wrap myself around him, and feel peace again. Confrontation wasn't something I reveled in, and being surprised by Victoria like this left me feeling disconcerted.

Victoria's gaze flickered between River and me, the air crackling with her sudden shift in demeanor. "Oh. My. God. You two are fucking, aren't you?" The words slithered out of her mouth, venomous and sharp. "I knew it," she spat, eyes narrowing with a triumph that made my skin crawl. "All the time you spent together. I always suspected there was something…off. Best friends, my ass."

River stood beside me, his calm exterior showing nothing of what he might be feeling inside.

"Did you plan this all along, River? Waiting in the wings like some pathetic vulture, ready to swoop in the moment my back was turned?" she continued.

"Victoria, stop," I interjected, but she barreled on, relentless.

"Or did you seduce him? Take advantage of his vulnerability?" She stepped closer to River, who held his ground despite the onslaught. "How does it feel to be someone's second choice?"

Each word Victoria hurled felt like a blow, and I could see the muscles in River's jaw tense. He exhaled slowly, a measured breath of restraint, but his silence was louder than any defense he could have offered.

"Enough, Victoria," I said, stepping in front of River. Her words might have been aimed at him, but they pierced me just as deeply.

She lifted her chin in defiance. "I guess I have all I needed from tonight." She stormed away, her dress swishing as she moved, never losing her poise.

It took a moment for my blood pressure to return to a semi-normal level before it shot up again.

"River," I said, "she's going to tell everyone. Spin it into some twisted tale."

As the thought formed in my head, a knot formed in my throat with the realization of how quickly she could unravel us.

All the times we innocently hung out at his place watching a game. Or when we went to Tanner's with my brothers. She could even spin those late nights I worked alone in the office.

I reached for him, finding relief in his familiar gaze. Our lips met, and for a fleeting moment, the world around us ceased to exist.

"Adam," he whispered against my mouth, pulling back just enough to meet my gaze. "I don't care what she says. You and I know our truth. That's all that matters."

I wanted to believe that, but with the blinders off, I could no longer make excuses for Victoria. She would do this out of spite, and suddenly, I would no longer be the jilted groom. I'd be the cheater she finally found the courage to leave.

Wasn't she brave? It must have been heartbreaking to find out her fiancé was cheating on her. And with a man, nonetheless.

That's what people would say.

I couldn't let her ruin our reputations. "I have to go after her, River. I can't let her control the narrative. This is our story." My hands lingered on his arms, tracing the outlines of his tattoos under his rolled-up sleeves.

"Go." He nodded, a gentle firmness in his tone. "But, Adam, remember we're more than whatever she—or anyone else—says."

"Thank you," I said, gratitude lacing my voice. With one last look at him, I promised, "I'll see you at home later."

"You better."

Then, I turned on my heel and ran toward the parking lot, determined to catch Victoria before she could weave her web of lies.

31

ADAM

"ADAM!" Lex's voice cut through my determination to get to my car. "Hey, wait up!"

I turned to see him jogging toward me, his expression etched with concern.

"What's up?" I asked, forcing a smile I didn't feel.

"We saw Victoria." He paused in front of me, his breaths coming out in quick puffs. "What happened?"

His question hung in the air, and for a brief moment, I considered shrugging it off, but this was Lex, my twin, the only person apart from River who knew me inside and out.

"She came to talk," I began, the words tasting bitter on my tongue. "But things… didn't go as planned."

Lex's brow furrowed, and he crossed his arms, a silent invitation to continue.

"Victoria, she…" I trailed off, the confession clawing at my throat. "Let's just say she's made some assumptions about River and me."

"Like what?"

"She thinks I cheated on her."

"That's bullshit," he said, raising his voice.

"I know, but she can do a lot of damage with that lie, and she doesn't get to take my coming out away from me."

"Damn." Lex exhaled. "I'm sorry, man. You okay?"

I nodded. "I'll deal with it. Right now, I need to ensure she doesn't cause any more trouble."

"Be careful, Adam. Don't let her get to you. You know we all have your back, right?"

"Always," I said.

With a final pat on my shoulder, Lex stepped back.

I ran toward my car, hoping I was right about where she was.

I hesitated at the doorstep of what was once my forever home, my fingers trembling as they hovered over the doorbell.

The door swung open, and there she stood, Victoria, her expression a mix of surprise and something unreadable. For a moment, neither of us spoke.

"Adam," she said, her voice tentative. "I…wasn't expecting you."

"Can I come in?"

"Of course." She stepped aside.

As I crossed into the living room, the memories of laughter and planning a life together seemed like the ghosts of a past life. The couch where we'd cuddled, made out, and had sex on was just a couch. The walls that were to be lined with pictures of our life together stood bare.

It was surreal, standing there amid the remnants of a life I thought I wanted.

I sat on the couch and tried to measure my words.

"You said you got what you came for at the botanical gardens, but I didn't get the same privilege," I said.

"What do you mean?"

"Why did you leave me on our wedding day? What was so terrible that you couldn't talk to me?" The question clawed its way out after weeks of gnawing at me from the inside.

She shifted uncomfortably, looking at anything but me. Her hands fidgeted, betraying the calm exterior she tried to project. When her gaze finally met mine, I saw a flicker of something raw and unguarded before she quickly masked it.

"Adam, I am so sorry," she whispered. "I made a mistake."

"What kind of mistake?"

"I…um…with…Liam Harper. It was just a slip, an error in judgment," she quickly added.

"To use your own words, you *fucked* our wedding caterer?"

"It wasn't—"

I help up a finger. "Mistakes are spilled milk or forgotten anniversaries. You didn't trip and fall on his dick by accident."

"Well, when you put it like that."

I laughed. "Is there another way to put it?" And then I took a breath. "Victoria, we need to rewind a little because, an hour ago, you called me a cheater, and now you're telling me this."

"Do you remember the family brunch? The one where you turned up with River hungover and barely able to string a sentence together without wincing?"

I cringed. "Of course I do." That had been one of the few times I'd been out with River in months and things had gotten a little out of hand. Despite everything, I was still angry with myself for getting that drunk before a family event. "But what does that have to do with you riding Liam's fun stick?"

She rolled her eyes. "Don't be childish."

"You just told me you cheated on me after accusing me of cheating on you. I'm going to be however I want to be."

Victoria did a double-take as if she wasn't expecting me to stand up for myself. I pushed that information to the back of my mind and gestured for her to continue.

"That brunch was a nightmare. The looks of pity I got because of you were beyond embarrassing. I bumped into Liam a couple of weeks later at a work function he was catering for. I didn't know he would be there. We had a drink together afterward and mostly talked about plans for the wedding, but…"

"At some point, you went from discussing cocktail sticks to him showing you his."

"Yes," she said, sounding exasperated. "Look, I wasn't in a good place. Work was stressing me out, your family hated me—"

"Don't you dare put this on my family, Victoria. No one made you cheat."

"No, that's true."

"How long did it go on for?"

"I broke it off immediately, Adam," she said, her voice a quiet plea for understanding. "It was just once."

"Then why didn't you tell me earlier? Why did you wait until the wedding day?"

"He came to talk to me the night before the wedding." Her gaze dropped, unable to meet mine. "He wanted us to be together."

"What?"

"I couldn't do it," she added quickly. "But the moment I considered it, I knew I couldn't marry you. If I could think about being with someone else…then maybe I didn't love you enough to make that kind of commitment."

"Are you with him now?"

"No." She shook her head. "It's over. It never really started."

"Why did you do it? Did I miss the signs that you were unhappy?"

She sighed. "I didn't know I was unhappy until I voiced it to Liam. I didn't even know I was capable of cheating. But…I was tired of trying to fit in with your family and failing. I felt it every time we were together. It was like I was always on the outside. I tried so hard, you know? Your family, your friends…I did everything I thought I should, but it never felt like enough. It's like they never really liked me."

Her admission hung in the air, raw and vulnerable. Had that really been her experience? I thought about it.

The disappointment on my mom's face when Victoria refused to try her casserole because the meat looked too fatty. Or how my dad tried so hard to find common ground by asking Victoria about her hobbies and she said she was too busy at work to have hobbies. I'd witnessed it the other way around. Victoria was the one who didn't seem to like my family despite how hard they tried to welcome her.

"Victoria, fitting into a family isn't about a checklist of things you do. It's a constant effort, yeah, but it's more about showing your love and being open to receiving it. After the first Sunday lunch with my family, during which you barely ate anything, you refused to join us for months. You never made a secret of your dislike for River, whatever the reason. What did you expect? To start baking cakes and fall into the family dynamics like you'd been there all along?"

"Okay, yeah, I admit it was a learning curve. I never understood your whole family being in each other's pockets. It was like we could never make plans on a Sunday because you always had to do the family thing."

I stared at her. "I'm not going to apologize for loving my family or for how close we are."

"River isn't family, is he?"

"What's with you and River? What's he ever done to you to deserve such animosity?"

Her expression faltered. "I was jealous," she admitted, her gaze dropping to her hands. "Of him. Of how he always seemed to be your priority."

"Jealous?"

"Yeah. All you ever talked about was River this and River that. We couldn't even have a movie night without you mentioning him."

"Did you think...?" I trailed off, unable to finish the thought. The accusation that might follow.

She looked up, her eyes meeting mine again. "It seems I had reason to."

"River has been my best friend all of my life. I don't care if you believe me or not, but nothing happened between us until after you left."

"How did it happen then? Did you wake up gay one day?"

"Not that I need to justify it to you or anyone else, but I've not labeled myself. I might be bisexual, pansexual, or one of the many queer identities. It doesn't matter. River was there for me when I needed him, and at some point, the way I saw him shifted into something I didn't expect or see coming."

She exhaled a long breath. "I believe you, and I'm sorry for what I said before...about River and you." She paused, her gaze dropping before finding mine again. "I wish you all the best. And who knows? Maybe there'll be another wedding for you to plan soon."

"What do you mean?" I asked, laughing.

"Don't you see it? You're so desperate to have the house

with the white picket fence and the two-point-five children that you ignore all the red flags. You did it with me, and if you don't pay attention, you'll do it with River."

"Are you saying River is a red flag?" What the fuck?

"Not him," she said. "The way you need other people is. You… You're the red flag, Adam."

That stopped me cold. I was the problem? Not her betrayal, not her secrets, but me and my need for something more in my life? My breath hitched, and I felt like the ground beneath me was shifting, unsteady.

"Victoria," I started, but the words lodged in my throat. There was nothing left to say. She had made her choice, and now, she had made her point.

"Goodbye, Victoria," I said finally. I stood and left the house without a single look back. I didn't take a breath until I was in my car.

I drove aimlessly at first, the city lights blurring. Victoria's words echoed in my head. Red flags. Desperation. The accusation stung because I was afraid she was right. Was I jumping from one wrong relationship into another?

Last time, I'd lost Victoria, but I still had my family and my best friend. If things didn't work out with River, who would I have left?

I wouldn't lose my family, but a split would be as hard for them as it would be for me. River would also lose a family, which wasn't fair to him.

There was no going home now, not with the storm of emotions threatening to engulf me. So, on autopilot, I found myself pulling up to Lex's house.

All the lights were off, so maybe they weren't home yet from the event. I pulled out my phone and called Lex.

"Adam?" he answered sleepily. His voice was laced with confusion. "What's up? It's late."

Fuck, how long had I been driving around?

"Can I crash at your place?" My voice was hoarse, almost foreign to my own ears.

"Of course," he said without hesitation, and I could hear the concern threading his tone.

When I reached his door, it swung open before I could knock. Lex stood there, his hair tousled from sleep, wearing an old Cliffborough High sweatshirt.

"Come here," he said softly, pulling me into a grounding hug. "Talk to me," Lex urged.

His place was a reflection of his great love story. The walls that had been bare months ago before Emery came back into his life were now filled with photos again.

My brothers gave me hope that great love was possible. Even Noah, who seemed to have sworn off it, was now more than happily married. He'd showed me that when you found your person, you could have your world flipped upside down and be happier for it.

I sank onto the couch, the leather cool against my skin. Lex sat beside me, close enough to be comforting yet giving me space to breathe.

"I spoke to Victoria. She said things about me, about River, but mostly me. She cheated, Lex. And now she's saying I'm…I'm the problem. That I hold on too hard and don't see the red flags."

"Adam," he said, his voice steady. "Wanting to love and be loved isn't a red flag. "River has been your safe harbor in all the times you've needed him. Maybe what's happening is the culmination of years of building your relationship."

"But that's the thing. How can I be sure I didn't just fall into his bed because I was hurt and had no one else? How do I know it's real? How do I not hurt him?" My throat threatened to close up as my thoughts spiraled in the wrong direction.

"Hey. First, listen to your heart, not what that woman

said. Second, get some rest," Lex said, standing to fetch a blanket. "We'll figure this out in the morning."

"Thanks," I murmured as he draped the blanket over me.

As Lex retreated to his room, I closed my eyes, not to sleep, but to picture River's face, his smile, his body, his kindness, his sense of humor, his taste in music.

Before sleep took me under, I had enough presence of mind to send him a message.

ADAM

I'm at Lex's. Can we talk tomorrow after your shift?

His reply came immediately, and the thought that he might have been waiting by his phone for me to call upset me. I felt bad for causing him to worry, but also happy that I still had someone who cared that much.

RIVER

Of course. Are you okay?

ADAM

I will be.

32

———

RIVER

THE CLINK of dishes and the murmur of happy patrons should have been music to my ears, especially after last night's successful fundraiser. Yet, there I stood, behind the bar, barely registering the bustle around me.

"River, man, what's with the long face?" Drew's voice cut through the sounds of the dining floor, his brow creasing in concern. He leaned against the counter, the sleeves of his white shirt rolled up to his elbows. "Last night was epic. People wouldn't stop talking about the food. You should be riding a victory lap right now, but you look like you were served shrimp scampi when you were expecting lobster tail."

I managed a halfhearted shrug. "I guess I'm just tired, you know. It was a big night for everyone. I half expected you to call off tonight. You and West must be run off your feet managing all those donations."

He grinned wide. "We're going to be pretty busy. Last night blew my mind."

"Saw you got a nice bid too"

He laughed. "Yeah. Who knew cocktail lessons would be so popular?"

It probably wasn't so much the cocktail lessons that got him the generous winning bid but the way the bidder seemed spellbound by Drew's charm on stage when he answered the questions from the emcee.

Any other time, I'd have teased him about it, but I wasn't even in the mood for that.

"Why don't you take a break? Looks like you need it, and from where I'm standing, the team has got it all under control."

He was right. I slipped past the servers and the kitchen crew into my office. Inside, I slumped into my chair, letting the silence envelop me. My mind replayed last night's events.

Adam's smile and barely-there nod that had been just for me when he was on stage. The way his smile fell when he saw Victoria. Her venomous comments. His absence.

All of our lives, he'd always come to me in times of need. I'd always been the safe space where he could work things through, and recently, what he'd been working through had been a lot to take in for anyone.

But last night, he sought his twin brother, not me.

"Argh. This is useless." I turned my computer off and grabbed my keys. On the way out, I asked Fir if he could keep an eye on the restaurant. He was, of course, more than happy to step up. Fir was a great guy and an excellent assistant manager. Lusitana couldn't be in better hands in my absence.

As I drove home, I knew I had to face the truth no matter how uncertain the outcome.

Lying to myself and to Adam would be denying us the best chance to be happy.

The door creaked as I nudged it open, the familiar, comfortable scent of my apartment wrapping around me.

Adam wasn't home yet.

I shuffled through the living room, past the couch where

we'd spent countless hours talking, listening to music, buried in a book, or laughing.

Crossing the room, I approached the cabinet where I kept all the important paperwork. I slid the drawer open and riffled through the contents until I found the envelope.

I lifted it out. Beneath the flap, neatly folded paper carried words I'd written but never shared. It was the decision I'd made before Adam's wedding and had been determined to execute until Adam's world flipped upside down, and as a result, so did mine.

The noise of the keys in the door announced Adam's return. I tucked the letter in my back pocket and glanced up, my breath catching as he emerged from the hall. He wasn't wearing the suit he had on yesterday, so I assumed the pair of jeans and shirt I didn't recognize were probably Lex's.

"Hey," Adam said, his voice low, the usual warmth replaced with a weary rasp.

"Hey," I echoed. The sight of him so visibly spent pulled at something deep within me. It was clear he hadn't found rest last night any more than I had.

Adam's eyes met mine, and I saw the shadows beneath them. His hair was tousled, likely from running his fingers through it. Whatever conversation he'd had with Victoria, it had left its mark.

He took slow steps toward where I stood, rooted to the spot. As soon as he was within reaching distance, I wrapped him in a tight hug. He turned his head to face me, and it hit me again, the same way I knew it would for the rest of my life, how much I fucking loved this man.

I'd tried to talk myself out of it. It was a crush. Much like the grass always seems greener on the other side, I'd hoped that having Adam reciprocate my affection wouldn't feel as perfect as it had in my head.

I'd been wrong. So fucking wrong.

"I talked to Victoria," he began, pausing to gauge my reaction.

"Okay," I replied cautiously.

"It clarified a lot of things for me," he admitted.

"Adam…"

He paused, his eyes meeting mine with a mixture of weariness and expectancy. "What is it?"

With a resolve that felt precarious at best, I reached into my back pocket. The paper crinkled as I drew it out. "Before you go on," I began, "there's something you need to know." My hand trembled slightly as I offered him the letter.

Adam took the envelope with a furrowed brow. He unfolded the letter, eyes scanning the words I'd penned in a moment of courage that now seemed like a distant memory.

As he read, his expression shifted, confusion knitting his brows. He looked up at me. "River, this is a resignation letter. You're leaving Lusitana?"

"No…or not right now."

"Then why do you have this?"

I began, my voice barely above a whisper, "Before your wedding, I…I made a decision." My gaze found his, holding steady. "I was planning to leave the restaurant and Cliffborough."

His eyes widened slightly, and I saw the gears turning behind the deep blue.

"Leave? For what?"

"Travel. I planned to explore the world, see new places, taste new foods. I wanted to open myself up to opportunities."

"You don't think you have opportunities here?" he asked.

"Not the kind I needed." My laugh was short, self-deprecating. "It was the only solution I could think of to find a way to cope…move on."

"Cope? With what?" He leaned in, concern etching lines around his eyes.

"With you getting married," I said, pushing past the lump in my throat. "With Victoria. With the thought of you belonging to someone else completely."

The silence that followed was heavy. I watched as understanding dawned, as he realized the depth of what I'd been hiding beneath the surface of our everyday interactions.

"River," he breathed out, and there was a world of emotion in the way he said my name. It sounded like a plea, a question, and a revelation all at once.

"After the wedding, I thought I would never need to use this letter. But last night, seeing you with Victoria, not knowing what would happen today... I realized you need to know the truth. I don't want to hide this from you, and I know I might lose you, but I'm also not going to let you go without a fight."

"Truth? About what?"

"About how much you mean to me, Adam. From the moment we met, you've been my everything. First, you were my friend, then the first person I came out to. We grew up, and all of a sudden, whenever you laughed, my belly tightened. I noticed how beautiful you were." I brought my hand up to cradle his cheek. "I noticed how sometimes you bite your nails when trying to figure out what to say or how your hair never seems to stay as tidy as Lex's, even when it starts out the same. I love you, Adam. I have for so long that I don't remember what it's like to not love you."

A small tear fell down his cheek. I leaned over and kissed it, tasting the salty liquid on my tongue.

"I'm sorry," I said. "I understand that your conversation with Victoria may have changed things for you, so you need to know that what we've been doing hasn't meant nothing to me. It's meant the fucking world. It's been the sip of water I've been searching for in the desert I've lived in for years."

33

———

ADAM

"You were going to walk away from everything? From me?"

"Only because I needed to try," River continued, his voice steady now, "to find somewhere new, start fresh, and maybe—just maybe—get my heart to beat for someone else."

"And yet," I pressed, needing to understand, "you stayed. Why?"

"Victoria left, and you needed me." His admission hung between us.

He was right. I'd needed him. I would always need him, and that was the problem.

"River," I managed to choke out, my voice barely above a whisper.

"You don't have to say you love me. You don't even have to feel it. But I need to breathe again. Being with you these last few weeks has been everything. If that's all I'll ever get, that's okay, but you'll need to let me go and move on. If there's even a small part of you that feels the same, then I'll stay and fight for you, Adam."

I gazed into his eyes, into his truth. River had never

245

asked me anything. He'd given me his support and his love freely. I thought I'd given it back, but my love had been wrapped in friendship because I'd been blind.

The realization cascaded through me, washing away any lingering doubt. I loved him. I loved River Hartley with an intensity that eclipsed anything I had ever felt for another soul, including Victoria.

I closed the distance between us. River's breath caught as I reached for him, my arms encircling his steady frame. Our lips met, and the kiss was a revelation. It was more than finding out I liked kissing men, specifically this one man. It was more than an awakening or something that had lain dormant inside me, waiting for the right time.

As my mouth moved against his, I poured every unspoken word, every hidden desire into that single moment.

River's hands came up to rest on my back, tentative at first, then with growing certainty as he returned my kiss with a need that matched my own. I placed my hand on the back of his neck, holding tight, memorizing the taste of his lips, the softness of his tongue.

It wasn't just a kiss. It was the beginning of everything.

My grandmother once said that new beginnings also bring new ends. The end can feel like a loss, but when we open our hearts to the world, the world will bring us new opportunities.

The kiss tapered off into nothing more than our lips joined together and our breaths mingling in the space between us.

River's eyes searched mine. "Adam, why did that feel like a goodbye kiss?"

His vulnerability, raw and exposed, struck me more than any blow could.

"Do you trust me?" I asked.

"Of course."

The weight of what I was about to say pressed down on me like a boulder. "I need to move out." The words hung between us, stark and undeniable.

He blinked, a frown creasing his brow. "If that's…what you want." His voice was practically a whisper, but I heard the resignation and grief he tried to hide.

"When I came in, I didn't have a plan. I knew I needed to see you and hoped I'd know the right thing to do."

"And you know now?"

I smiled, reaching for his face and caressing the short scruff.

"The words you want to hear, River, I want to say them. I feel them so fucking deep that I'm so close to calling off this whole 'needing space to figure myself out' idea."

"Then stay. I can give you space here. You can move back to the spare room. We barely see—"

I shut him up with my mouth, letting my lips linger on his a little longer than I wanted. This was going to be so fucking hard.

"River," I said when I pulled away. "When I started reading your romance books, you said the part you hate the most is when the guys break up before the end."

"Yeah. You called it the third-act breakup or some shit. I think you just wanted to show off your English degree smarts."

I laughed. "Yes, that's right. This is it, except there's no breakup. It's just a pause, okay? The conversation with Victoria forced me to face some truths about myself." The admission tasted bittersweet on my tongue. "And I need some time to work through it all. You deserve the best of me, and I can't be the best for you if I don't trust myself."

Understanding dawned in his eyes, but it did nothing to ease the tension that wired his frame.

"You've already done so much for me," I continued, each word etched with the guilt of a thousand apologies. "But I have to make one more selfish request. Will you wait for me?"

"As long as you need."

Those five words were everything. I had no doubt I would come back to him, but if I didn't stand on my own two feet, I would never be the man River deserved.

"Thank you," I managed to choke out.

As I stepped back, putting physical distance between us, I held on to the trust he placed in me. He would be here, waiting for my return.

He followed me as I went to his room—our room—and filled a duffel bag with as many clothes as I could fit, not particularly caring if they were mine or his.

"Adam," his voice finally broke through.

My hands trembled as I drew the zipper closed. I hoisted the bag over my shoulder, the weight of it less than the burden of walking away, yet somehow more meaningful.

"It's just a pause," I repeated, more as a reassurance to myself than anything.

"Where will you stay?"

"I'll be with Lex and Emery."

I stopped by the door and turned around. I didn't want to do this, but I needed to.

"I love you," he said.

I love you too.

RIVER

I STARED at the cooling coffee in the mug in front of me. It didn't taste the same anymore. Nothing did.

I used to crave my days off, but now my apartment felt too empty without Adam. I glanced at my phone again, but I knew if I went to work, Fir would follow through on his promise to change all the locks in the restaurant at his own cost.

But what the fuck could I do at home on my own? I didn't feel like reading because I would want to talk to Adam about it. I didn't feel like cooking because I couldn't save the leftovers for him.

Was that the reason he'd left? Did he feel like he needed space from me?

He said it was to figure himself out, but what if I was the problem?

I stood and dropped the mug in the sink.

You just miss him. You promised you'd wait, so grow a fucking pair and go out there and get some fresh air.

It had been a month since Adam left. Four weeks, and we'd only seen each other when he met his parents for lunch at the restaurant once. I'd watched him from afar, too afraid to get any closer and end up begging him to come back.

Drew had been a true friend and had reassured me Adam seemed okay.

We'd exchanged text messages, and sometimes it was like nothing had happened, while other times, I could tell he was still working through stuff.

I couldn't complain that I had no communication with him, but I needed more than words on a screen.

I'd promised to fight for him, but what had I done? I'd let him go, and I'd waited. I'd buried myself in work as if that could help fill the void where Adam should be.

A knock on the door, sharp and insistent, broke through my brooding thoughts. I hesitated before finally trudging toward the door. When I swung it open, Noah stood there, the familiar arch of his eyebrow conveying concern and impatience.

"You're not wearing that," he said.

I looked down at my T-shirt, jogging bottoms, and bare feet. "I'm definitely not naked, so yes, I am wearing this. What are you doing here?"

He pushed past me and down the hallway to my bedroom.

"Noah. What the fuck is going on?" I asked.

"You're getting dressed. That's what the fuck is going on. And then you're coming with me."

I groaned. "If this is some kind of intervention from you and Lex, you can drop it. It's all good. Adam is coming back, and it's all good."

"Yeah, it's all good. You said that twice."

"Because it's true." He opened and closed drawers until he seemed to find something suitable. I wanted to laugh because he'd picked Adam's favorite pair of jeans. I knew that because every time he wore them, he'd complain about the small tear on the knee, which stopped him from wearing them as part of a dressy-casual outfit.

Noah crossed his arms and stared at me.

When he wouldn't budge, I dropped my jogging bottoms.

"What the fuck, dude? You're naked," he said, covering his eyes.

"You're in my room demanding I get dressed. I'm getting dressed."

After he made a comment about the size of my junk and how lucky his brother was, I locked myself in the bathroom across the hall and got dressed. Pervert.

I didn't know what his deal was or what kind of intervention he, and probably Lex, had planned, but knowing the Spencer brothers, there wasn't much I could do about it.

"Where are we going?" I asked when I came out of the bathroom.

"Just trust me," he replied with the same smile he had when scheming. I wanted to say if he was going to force Adam to see me, he needed to learn how to respect his brother's wishes, but then again, I was also desperate to see Adam, so maybe I could go along for the ride.

When I slid into the passenger seat of his car, he handed me a black fabric blindfold.

"Are you serious?"

"It's payback time for when you all made me renew my vows with Lior with flat hair after kidnapping me."

"I didn't kidnap you. Drew and West did. Besides, your hair looked fine," I countered, but the protest fell on deaf ears.

"Put it on."

With a resigned sigh, I complied, darkness enveloping me as the soft fabric settled over my eyes. The absence of sight left me feeling vulnerable. But hey, at least it was a distraction from thinking about how much I missed Adam or how I wouldn't put it past Noah to drop me in the middle of a field with a bottle of water and a note saying dinner was on him if I made it home.

"Here, these will keep you company," Noah said, pressing a pair of earbuds into my palm. I fumbled to fit them into my ears, and as soon as they were snugly in place, music flooded through them.

Five songs played until the car finally came to a stop, pausing the playlist.

"We stopped?" I asked. "Can I take this blindfold off?"

"Yep, we're here." Noah's voice held a measure of excitement that put me on edge. "You can take it off now."

I reached up to remove the blindfold, ready to face whatever Noah, and probably Lex, had schemed up.

When my eyes adjusted to the light, I took in the familiar building in front of us and then looked at Noah. "Seriously, Noah, you brought me to work on my day off. Thanks."

He came out of the car and circled it before opening my passenger door. "Like you said, you're not working today. Today, you're the guest of honor."

"I'm what?" He practically dragged me out of the car and toward the Lusitana.

Inside, the restaurant buzzed with energy. People were everywhere, the tables had been rearranged, and music, which sounded like a continuation of the playlist I'd been listening to in the car, played in the background.

I recognized a few of my favorite regulars, some friends, and standing by the bar, Adam's parents' smiles were like twin beacons cutting through the sea of faces.

Had I missed some sort of celebration on the calendar?

As if on cue, Noah suddenly left my side, the music halted, and the crowd parted, making their way around the decorated tables and leaving the middle hallway, which was usually filled with servers going in and out of the kitchen, empty.

This time, there were no servers. No bells ringing in the kitchen.

Adam stood at the other end, holding on to a chair beside him.

My heart thrummed against my ribcage, its rhythm loud in my ears. My palms grew moist, and I discreetly wiped them on my jeans.

Adam's blue eyes found mine across the distance, and I saw his chest expand as he took a deep breath.

He stood on the chair, taking me back to the last time he'd done the same thing.

It felt like the whole room held its breath as Adam's voice trembled through the restaurant.

"Life," he began, "is a series of moments where you must decide whether to hold on or let go." In a room full of faces, his gaze never left me.

"Sometimes," Adam continued, his voice gaining strength, "you find parts of yourself in places you never thought to look. And sometimes, you're lucky enough to explore those newfound places with someone who makes you feel safe."

The crowd listened, enraptured by his words, unaware of what they meant.

"These past months have been a journey," he continued, "one where I've learned about bravery. About the courage it takes to face the truth that some things are beyond repair. But the hardest battles," he insisted, "are the ones that matter most."

A murmur of agreement passed through the onlookers, but for me, there was only Adam and the words spoken just for me.

"I found feelings within me, vibrant and undeniable. Feelings I navigated with the one person who has always been my compass, my confidant, my best friend." He stepped down from the chair and took a few steps forward.

I swallowed and pressed my hands against my sides because they shook so much.

"River," he said, and hearing my name on his lips in such a tender manner sent shivers down my spine, "you've been safeguarding a piece of me—a piece I didn't even realize I'd given away. Somehow, without intent or expectation, you had my heart all this time. Maybe even before I knew it was beating for you."

I took a slow step forward, afraid to break our connection.

"Keep it," he said, "Keep my heart because without you close, every breath feels borrowed, every moment half-lived."

"Adam…" I whispered, but I didn't think it came out at all.

"I needed to step back, to figure out if I sought you because you were there or if it was because it was always meant to be you. You deserve someone who loves you whole-heartedly and undoubtedly. I've listened to all our songs and reread all our books. I have nothing left. No more doubts that what I feel for you is real and everlasting."

The crowd erupted in soft applause. Adam Spencer, with his piercing blue eyes and heart laid bare, had chosen to stand before everyone we knew and declare his love.

I navigated the sea of faces, each step carrying me closer to him. Standing before him, I could see the subtle tremor in his hands, the vulnerability only I'd been privileged to see. In one fluid motion, I lifted him, and he wrapped his legs instinctively around my waist.

Crowd or no crowd, I needed him. Our lips met in a kiss

that was the culmination of every moment that had led us here. It was messy and filled with emotion.

"And this is why there's a fucking third-act breakup in romance novels," he said when I finally let him come up for air. The crowd around us be damned. They could look away.

I laughed. "I missed you so fucking much, Adam."

His eyes held mine with an intensity that left no room for doubt. "God, I've missed you too. And in case it wasn't clear in my amazing speech, I love you."

"Your amazing speech, huh?" I chuckled. He slid down to his feet, which released my hands, allowing me to cradle his face and run my thumbs over his lower lip. "I love you too, baby."

Our bubble burst when we were surrounded by Adam's brothers, their partners, and then their parents and grandmother.

"We're so happy for you both," Carla said, pulling me in for a hug. "You know, I always wondered if you two would ever be together, but I just thought I'd gotten it wrong. It seems my mother instincts were right."

"You could have given me the heads-up, Mom," Adam said.

"You have to figure these things out for yourself, honey."

Adam stared back at me. "I was a little slow on the uptake, but I intend on making up for lost time."

The next twenty minutes felt like three hundred weeks that we spent receiving congratulations from people, hearing how cute we looked together, and smiling through all the wedding questions.

Every time I glanced at Adam, I could tell he was getting tired of it.

His hand never left mine, so at the earliest opportunity, I pulled him toward the kitchen. I used an excuse I didn't buy myself, so I didn't expect our friends to buy it, but they didn't say anything.

"This is a great party and all, but I am familiar with the quality of the food, and there's no one in that crowd I'm dying to get naked with. Do we have to stay?" I pulled Adam closer and buried my face in his neck, sucking lightly on his skin. Enough to rile him up but not leave a mark.

He glanced around at the gathered crowd. Shaking his head, a playful smirk danced on his lips. "They'll manage without us. Come on, let's go out through the back door," he urged, his grin the very definition of joy as he tugged me toward the door.

We made an almost clean escape before bumping into Fir.

"Dammit," he said. "Just lost twenty bucks."

"What?"

"There was a bet going around the staff. I said you'd last an hour. Drew bet on twenty minutes. Chef said you'd last two hours, but I think it's because he thinks no one can resist his food."

I laughed. "Sorry about that. I'll make it up to you with an extra day off."

"No need, boss. Go be happy with your man."

I looked at Adam. "That's the plan."

35

———

ADAM

I COULDN'T STOP myself from stealing another kiss before I left River in the passenger seat of my car. I was a parched man, and River was the drink I craved.

"Where are we going?" he asked when I started the car.

"The hotel downtown. You know as soon as my brothers realize we're missing, they'll give us a couple of hours tops before they break into your place with an excuse that we need to go somewhere. The only place I need to be is inside you. Or you inside me. Those are the only two viable options for the next…week."

River chuckled softly, a sound that made the corner of my mouth turn up in a half-smile.

"Your brothers are weird."

"The apples don't fall far from the tree," I said.

"What do you mean?"

I stopped at a red light and glanced briefly at him. He took my hand and brought it to his mouth, placing a soft kiss on my palm.

"Last week, I met with my parents…to come out to them

257

and tell them about us. Well, I hoped there would still be an us."

"There will always be an us if it depends on me," River said. "I've already been without you enough to last a lifetime, so from now on, we're stuck like glue."

He chuckled. "How romantic."

"Anyway, you were telling your story."

"Yes. Do you remember Mom started saying something on my…on the wedding day, and she never finished?"

"Yeah, I remember that. What was that about?"

"So, Dad kidnapped Mom on their wedding day because he was afraid Mom's dad would stop them from getting married."

"He what?"

"Yup. He did. Mom convinced him to return to the venue and get married like a normal person. After the wedding, Dad told Mom that her dad had made some veiled threats. They spoke to Granddad, and as it turned out, it was all a ploy from Granddad to test Dad. If he ran with Mom, it meant he really loved her. If he ran away on his own, then it was a lucky escape for Mom."

"I bet your mom was super happy to know that."

"Grandma said Granddad was grounded for a while, but I didn't ask what that meant." I laughed.

"What am I getting into with you?" he said, but then his voice became softer. "You know we could've done this at my place, right? Saved you the grand gesture…"

I glanced at him. "Yeah, but then it wouldn't have been a grand gesture, would it? I needed everyone we know to see and understand what was happening between us and how special it was."

We stole heated glances all the way to the hotel. When we arrived, I left the car with the valet and grabbed our overnight bag. There was a lot to be said for River and me being practically the same size.

Inside, we walked past the reception desk toward the elevators. "I have the key already," I said.

River laughed. "Who knew you were such a Boy Scout."

As the elevator doors closed on us, I pushed him against the wall. "My motto is to always be prepared, and trust me, baby. I am more than prepared."

His Adam's apple bobbed at the realization of what I meant.

"Are you sure?" he asked, searching my face for absolute certainty.

"I've never been more sure of anything."

The lock on the door clicked, so I pushed it open to reveal the luxurious décor of the suite. Soft carpet, expensive paintings on the wall, floor-to-ceiling windows overlooking the city… It was the best suite the hotel had available.

None of it mattered because my eyes locked in on the large bed in the middle of the room. *That* was where I needed to be. With River. Naked.

I dropped the bag on the floor. River went straight to the window to admire the view. While he was distracted, I grabbed the lube and condoms, hoping we wouldn't need the latter.

"This is really nice, Adam. You know you didn't have to," he said. "I'd be happy in a less fancy place." He walked up to me. "A bed and four walls is all we need. Hell, we don't even need the bed."

I met him halfway, suddenly ravenous for his touch. The space between us evaporated as we bumped against the bed, my hands roaming over his body like they were making up for lost time.

"Adam…I lov—" His breath hitched as my lips found his neck.

"Say it again," I whispered.

"Adam," he repeated, his voice stronger this time, surer. "I love you."

The words crashed over me. River loved me, had always loved me, and every fiber of my being responded with an intensity that bordered on reverence.

Our bodies moved together, hungry and insistent.

"River," I gasped, pulling back just enough to drink in the sight of him, flushed and wanting. "I've been dreaming about this moment." I shook my head. "I'm almost scared of how much I want this."

He relieved me of my shirt, kissing my chest and licking my nipples until they were two pink pebbles, aching for more. "Years, Adam. I've wanted you for years…"

I pushed up on the bed, lying in the middle and opening my legs. River took the hint and covered my body with his, taking my mouth for a searing kiss.

"I got tested," I said, the words tumbling out like a confession. "I'm negative."

We'd never talked about not using condoms, but I'd gotten tested after we'd had sex and I came inside him in the condom. All I'd thought about after that was how I wanted nothing between us. The thought of my cum leaking out of his ass afterward had gotten me hard every time I thought about it.

"Are you sure?"

"I've never been so sure of anything. River, every single cell in my body wants you."

He groaned. "Fuck, Adam, you certainly know how to get a guy going."

"I sure hope so, but there's only one guy I'm interested in."

I flipped us so I was on top of him, and it was my turn to explore his skin, tasting the salt and heat of him as I made my way down his body. When my mouth encased his cock, taking him in, his groans became music to my ears.

"Tell me you're negative too," I said, running my tongue down his shaft, exploring the area leading to his hole. I'd also been researching rimming and other ways of bringing pleasure to a man.

"Adam…" His hands fisted in the sheet as his hips bucked, seeking more. "I'm negative. Fucking fuck, you're killing me." He raised his head and pulled me up so we were face-to-face. "I got tested after the last time I had sex with someone… It's been a while since."

"Really? How long?"

He groaned. "Can we not talk about it?"

"You've piqued my curiosity."

"Eighteen months, okay? It was after you told me how serious you were about Victoria. There was this guy I'd been talking to. We got along well so I hoped maybe he could turn into the one, you know? Newsflash, he wasn't the one."

"Because the sex was bad?" I teased.

"No, you fucker, because there's only ever been one *the one*, and that's you. Now pass me the lube so I can take that smug look off your face."

I laughed. "You think having your fingers and your dick in my ass will remove my smug smile? Baby, welcome to Adam 2.0, the bi-edition."

He grabbed the lube from the bedside table and placed it by the pillow, then he held my hands, pinning them above my head and kissing me gently.

"You found a label?" he asked.

"Not really. I'm toying with a few different ones, but it's not easy because, until you, I had no interest in men."

"Ahh," he said, "the magic dick."

"The what?" I laughed.

"The magic dick that turns straight men gay, players into

straight-laced monogamous men. You know, in romance novels?"

"Oh my god." I almost cried from laughing. "You do not have a magic dick."

He wiggled his eyebrows. "Wanna bet?"

I wrapped my hand around his neck and pulled him in for a kiss. "It's what I'm here for. Now, let's stop talking and get down to business."

"Yes, sir," he whispered against my lips.

"Oh, I could get used to that."

He slapped my ass and then hooked my leg over his hip.

"I need to see you unravel, baby. Show me everything, okay?"

I nodded, swallowing dry as he coated his fingers with lube and massaged my rim.

"Keep going," I urged when his fingers probed deeper. "I've been…practicing," I admitted, feeling a blush creeping over my skin.

"What have you been doing?" he asked, his voice hoarse with lust.

"Using my fingers, toys…"

He growled like the thought of me practicing to be with him reached a level deep inside him.

"Baby, you make me so hard for you. Can you feel it?"

I nodded as he pressed his cock against my thigh. Thickness that would soon be filling me up.

My breath caught as he breached me with his fingers.

"I'll go slow, okay?" he reassured.

I nodded. "Not too slow."

I was already feeling the heat creep up my body. When I said I'd been practicing, I'd meant it. All the times Noah had waxed lyrical about prostate orgasms, I'd thought he was messing with me.

I'd already seen River's reaction to me pressing on his

prostate first-hand, but when I'd probed my little bundle of nerves with a toy I'd bought, I'd seen stars.

And then I'd counted myself lucky for having waited until Lex and Emery were out before I'd experimented because I hadn't been quiet.

"Adam," he whispered, his voice filled with awe. "Look at you. How you're taking my fingers so beautifully. You're going to love having my cock inside you, aren't you?"

"Fuck, yes." I couldn't wait. I pushed back against his fingers. "More, River, please," I pleaded, my fingers digging into his shoulders.

I felt the absence of his fingers, but soon, his lubed cock pressed against my hole. I relaxed, ready for the bigger intrusion.

River held my leg higher on his waist, opening me. "Next time we do this, I want to see my cock going in and out of your hole, baby. I want to see you stretching around me. But today, I want to see your face as I fill you with my cum."

"How is that dirty talk so fucking sexy?"

"Welcome to River 2.0, the boyfriend edition. I'm going to look after you so good, baby, you'll never want anyone else."

"Fuuuck…" I cried as he filled me slowly. It was so much better than the toys or my fingers.

River's eyes locked on my face just like he'd promised, so I didn't need to ask him to move because he read my body like it was his favorite book.

Heat coiled in my belly, passion spiraling out of control as we moved together, gasping and moaning.

"Fuck, Adam, you feel so good, so incredibly tight."

Our rhythm grew erratic, frenzied, as we chased the precipice that promised sweet oblivion. With each pass of River's cock over my prostate, I lost the ability to talk or even think. My body was coiled and ready to explode.

"River," I cried, unable to give him more than a few seconds warning.

He didn't stop thrusting in and out of me, drawing out my orgasm for what felt like forever, swallowing my cries with his mouth as he pushed in one last time and came inside me.

Afterward, we clung to each other, chests heaving, unwilling to let go, our eyes locked. Even as I felt River's release drip down my leg, there was no ick, no shame, just the rightness of having a little bit of my person inside me, and he had been my person in one way or another since we were five.

Lying in the tangled bedding, I traced the line of River's collarbone with a finger still trembling from exertion. The room was thick with the heady scent of sex, and the air conditioner hummed quietly. His chest rose and fell against mine in a comforting rhythm.

"Baby," he murmured, "does this mean you're moving back?"

"My bag is in the car already. If you're okay with moving this fast, I'd love to live with you."

He laughed. "Fast? Fast implies a suddenness, an unpreparedness. Adam, I've been ready since I discovered my sexuality wasn't just a part of who I am. It's intrinsically connected to you, Adam Spencer."

"Then let's not waste any more time," I whispered.

"But first, let's clean you up before we get permanently glued together."

"You say that like it's a bad thing."

I knew River would never stop looking after me because that was his love language. While I'd been away, I'd thought a lot about that. At first I didn't feel worthy, but now I got it. Those same words I'd said to Victoria also applied to me.

Belonging was about letting yourself be loved the same way you love.

We took our time in the shower, cleaning each other and catching up with information we'd missed. Apparently, something had happened between Drew and West after the charity auction.

Since I'd spent more of my time in the last month working or thinking about River and our future, I'd missed the aftermath of the event. I hoped the guys finally got past whatever was stopping them from being together because it was evident they loved each other.

When I thought about it, Drew and West reminded me of River and me. We'd built such a strong relationship that when something new came along, we were afraid it could break our foundation, except we were stronger than any shake-up.

We settled back in bed, facing each other, our smiles refusing to ease. River caressed my back while I traced the lines on his beautiful tattoos.

Both our phones rang at the same time, disturbing our peace. We laughed and grabbed them.

"I got Lex," I said.

"I have Noah."

I nodded for him to answer his phone and declined the call from Lex.

"Why are you fuckers not at your apartment?" Noah asked through the speakerphone.

"How do you know we're not at my place?" River asked, quirking a brow.

"Because…" He groaned. "Never mind."

Lex's voice came on the call. "You know this isn't fair, right?"

"You mean it's not fair we played you at your own game and won?" I asked.

"We're going to TP your apartment just for the sake of it," Noah said.

"Do we have to? I'd rather go to Margot's," Emery said in the background.

"I'm with Emery on this one," Lior added.

"Hey, guys," River said. "Sounds like it's an awesome party where you are, but we're going to give it a miss. Lock the door before you leave."

River hung up the call before they had a chance to reply.

We laughed for a solid minute before high-fiving each other.

"You realize we're unstoppable, right? They both recruited outsiders, but we're OG," I said.

We exchanged lazy kisses until my belly rumbled.

"Shall I grab the room service menu?" River asked.

"It's like you can read my mind."

"Or hear your belly…"

My eyes followed River, tracing each line of his body as he got out of bed to pick up the menu from the table in the sitting area facing the windows. Thank fuck we were high up and couldn't be seen.

When he came back to bed with the menu, he lay beside me, giving me a perfect view of the curves of his ass and back.

"I have a little confession to make," I said.

"Oh yeah?" he asked, turning back to me.

I bit my lip. "About my…the honeymoon trip."

"Okay…"

"The morning after we had dinner together at the beach restaurant, I woke up before you. You laid there sleeping so peacefully. I couldn't help taking in your body, the way the muscles in your back moved with each deep breath. Something shifted. I was so confused, and I ran to the bathroom. My dick was so hard I had to jerk off. Nearly had a heart attack when you called me from the bedroom because you needed to pee."

He stared at me with his mouth gaped.

"That's not all I did."

He raised a brow.

"I heard you one time."

"You heard me?"

"Jerking off…in the shower. You called my name. I think that was the point of no return. I became obsessed with you. I was also very confused and worried about doing something that would damage our friendship."

"But you still kissed me," he said, looking stupidly smug.

"You're pretty irresistible."

He pulled me closer, and I felt his dick rallying for round two, just like mine. "I guess we'll have to honeymoon in Maui to relive the old times," he said. "But this time, I get to watch you jerk off for me."

"Are you asking me what I think you're asking me, River Hartley?"

"Suck my dick like you want to do it for the rest of your life, and I'll tell you."

The room service menu was forgotten for a little longer while I showed my boyfriend exactly how I wanted to spend the rest of my life.

EPILOGUE

A Year Later

PART 1

—

LEX

I chuckled as I fumbled with the silver cufflinks, my fingers more clumsy than usual. Across the room, Emery laughed. "You're not wearing those on our wedding day, or I'll be waiting for you at the altar until I'm old enough to put in for retirement," he teased.

"That won't be a problem because I'll be getting ready in my own suite and won't be distracted by you making love to that ice cream wearing nothing but your underwear."

He shot me a heated gaze. "I could take them off." And then he licked the spoon, drawing it over his tongue. My dick hardened immediately. Not that difficult when I was around my fiancé.

"You're a tease," I said, stalking over to where he sat enjoying his favorite breakfast of pancakes with ice cream. I kneeled between his legs, took his spoon, and scooped it full of ice cream into my mouth. Before I swallowed, I pressed my lips against Emery's.

He moaned when I coaxed his mouth open and transferred the still-cold ice cream from my mouth to his.

"Hmm, you taste good, baby," I said, warming his cold lips with mine.

He responded with another moan, so I kissed him until I could no longer taste the ice cream, only the flavor of my favorite person.

"Can you believe we'll be doing this next summer?" Emery asked, his gaze catching mine as he ran his fingers through my hair. "Standing in front of everyone we love, making it all official?"

"Sometimes it feels surreal," I admitted. "Like a dream I'm afraid to wake up from because what if I do, and it turns out you're still gone?"

"Hey." He placed his hands on either side of my face. "I'm here, and we've made enough memories together to make up for the ones I've lost."

"I love you so fucking much, Emery."

"I love you too, Lex," he said after a moment, pulling back with a smile that promised forever. "Come on, let's get you buttoned up. Adam and River are counting on us to be ready." He stood, taking me with him.

"Says he who is practically naked."

He struck a pose with his hands on his hips and stuck his tongue out.

"Hey, do you think they'll resist not seeing each other before the ceremony?" Emery asked, his voice dancing with mischief as he leaned against the hotel room's dresser.

"I wouldn't."

"Is that so?" His laugh was a low rumble, sending a shiver of desire down my spine.

"That is so. And I wouldn't even break the rules."

"How?"

I winked. "I have my ways."

"Maybe I wouldn't let you in my suite. I'm a nice boy who follows the rules, you know?" he said.

It wasn't a lie, and I loved when he did all the right things, like driving his teacher colleague to an out-of-state conference just because she was scared of flying. I also fucking loved it when he broke the rules.

I crouched by my suitcase and searched for the tie I'd worn to the rehearsal dinner. "You'd beg me to break the rules, baby."

"Prove it."

I approached him, the silk tie sliding through my fingers like a promise. "Close your eyes," I instructed, my heart racing with every step.

He complied, and I blindfolded him with care, ensuring the fabric hugged his head just right, leaving him in darkness. His breath hitched, and the air between us became charged with an electric current.

"Lex..." Emery's voice was a blend of excitement and vulnerability.

"Shh," I whispered, tracing my fingers along his jawline before sinking to my knees. The scent of his body wash mingled with his arousal, intoxicating me further as I pulled his boxer shorts down to his knees and took him into my mouth.

The fact he was fully naked while I was already dressed—cufflinks and all—made it all the more electric between us.

"Ngh..." Emery's hands found my hair, his grip tight yet reverent. The sound of his restrained moans was sweeter than a song. "Oh fuck, Lex."

I pulled off him with a pop. "How can I be Lex? You can't see your groom before the ceremony, remember?"

He gasped as I resumed my worship of his cock, taking him down all the way until my mouth was full and he touched the back of my throat.

I massaged the inside of his legs with one hand while the other tugged his balls gently. He'd spill into my mouth in no time because I knew Emery's body better than my own.

As soon as I teased a single finger around his rim, I felt the tell-tale shakes of his impending orgasm.

"Lex, I—" His words broke off in a gasp as I brought him to the brink, his body tensing, seeking release.

When he finally came, it was with my name on his lips, a declaration that echoed in the stillness of the room as I drank every single drop of his essence.

I carefully undid the blindfold, revealing his flushed cheeks and the raw adoration in his eyes.

Without a word, he switched places with me, his mouth on mine, claiming me with a hunger that matched mine. As Emery returned the favor, my world narrowed to the sensation of him, the heat, and the pleasure only he could bring to me.

After I came, releasing his name with a hoarse cry, we stood holding each other, marveling over the connection we had.

"True love never forgets," he said, like he had almost two years ago when we got together again. His memories may never return, but his heart always knew it belonged to me.

"True love never forgets…" I repeated after him.

"Okay, time to get all dolled up for Adam and River's big day."

Since our detour hadn't left a mess, we picked up his suit and my jacket from the matching hanging bags and *finally* got ready.

"Look at us," Emery said, stepping closer until our reflections merged in the mirror. "Two handsome devils ready to charm the hell out of everyone." His hands found their way to my tie, adjusting it with deft fingers, the intimacy of the gesture making my heart skip a beat.

"Only you, baby." I caught his wrist, bringing his hand to my lips for a brief, tender kiss. "Only you could make me feel like the luckiest man alive just by fixing my tie."

His chuckle was a warm caress against my skin. "And only you could turn a simple wedding prep into something so damn poetic. I thought Adam was the wordsmith Spencer." He reached up to brush a rogue strand of hair from my forehead.

"I can make you a drawing if you like. It'll be me with permanent heart eyes, holding a bouquet of peonies for you."

"Do you think it'll be super hot outside?" Emery asked.

Adam and River had decided to marry at the same resort in Maui that we'd visited on his honeymoon. I hadn't been sure it was a good idea, but as Adam had said, that vacation had marked a new start in his life, which had taken him to River.

"The ceremony is inside, baby. We can come back to drop off our jackets before the beach reception."

A knock at the door made us jump, and I moved to answer it with a foreboding tightening my gut. The last time we heard an unexpected knock on the morning of a wedding, it had been River telling us Victoria had left.

The door swung open, revealing River, his face pale, eyes wide with panic, and my stomach sank.

"The rings—I can't find them anywhere," he gasped.

"Wait, Adam's not gone?"

He froze, his voice going a few octaves higher. "What? Adam's gone?"

"Guys," Emery said in his usual calm. "You're not listening to each other." Then he turned to River. "What's the problem?"

"You promise Adam's not gone?"

Emery smiled. "Promise."

River sighed in relief before his eyes found the panic setting again. "I can't find our wedding rings."

"How? When did you last have them?" I asked.

"I—I don't know," River stammered, his fingers raking through his hair. He was already dressed in his wedding suit, looking every bit the nervous groom. "I had them, I swear. I mean, I thought I had them in my suitcase, but I've looked everywhere…" His voice trailed off, lost in the gravity of what this meant.

"Okay, hey, breathe," I urged, stepping forward to place a steadying hand on his shoulder.

"We'll find them, all right?"

"Adam's going to kill me," River whispered, his usual calm demeanor shattered by the weight of the moment. It pained me to see him like this, unraveling at the seams, on his wedding day of all days.

"Adam won't care about the rings as much as he cares about you," Emery chimed in, his voice soothing. "We've got time before the ceremony. Let's think this through."

"Could they have fallen out somewhere?" I suggested, my mind racing through possibilities. "Maybe when you were getting ready?"

"Maybe," River conceded, though doubt clouded his eyes. "I checked my room already, tore it apart, but nothing."

"All right," I said, injecting confidence into my tone. "We split up. Search the places you've been since last having them. They have to be here, River. This place isn't that big, and we haven't left the resort."

"Okay." River nodded, his breathing steadier now. "I'll retrace my steps. Maybe…maybe I dropped them somewhere along the way."

"Good." I gave his shoulder a reassuring squeeze. "Emery and I will check the common areas, ask around. Someone might've seen something."

River's gaze flickered between us, gratitude mingling with the lingering fear. "Thank you," he murmured, the vulnerability in his voice tugging at my heart.

"Hey, no thanks needed," Emery replied, his smile gentle. "You'd do the same for us."

"First, we need backup. Let's grab Noah," I suggested, knowing that, if anything, Noah would help calm River down and inject a slice of humor.

"Good idea," River replied, the panic in his eyes beginning to subside.

PART 2

NOAH

I took a quick glance at the clock on the bedside table.

Plenty of time.

I was spread out on the bed like an offering, limbs tethered to the posts with silken restraints I'd found in the back of a kitschy adult store in Lahaina. The ties were a soft contrast to the firmness of Lior's touch, sending shivers down my spine.

"More," I whispered, never above begging, as Lior's tongue traced the sensitive expanse of skin behind my knees, working its way up my thighs with purposeful patience.

"You taste delicious, baby," he said, his voice a low growl that vibrated through me. "Like saltwater and sex."

I closed my eyes. "That's because you fucked me three ways into this morning before I died last night."

"I must not have done a very good job if you begged me for more the moment you opened your eyes this morning."

"Quite the opposite. You're so good, I can't get enough. Maybe you should try not being so good at sex." I yipped when I felt a bite on my ass cheek. "I take it back. Please don't ever be bad at sex because I really love it. With you. And I really love you."

He chuckled. "I love it when you beg like this, Noah." And then, with no more preamble than the tightening grip of his hands on my hips, he opened my ass cheeks and dove in, his tongue finding that spot that unraveled me completely.

My breath hitched, my body arching into the sensation as pleasure coiled tight within me. The world outside the four walls of our hotel room faded to nothing. There was only here, now, the unyielding press of his mouth, the sweet tension urging me toward that precipice.

"God, Lior…" The name fell from my lips like a prayer. This man knew exactly how to break me into little pieces, like the shards of glass from his stained-glass workshop.

The second release hit me harder than the first, a rush of white-hot intensity that left me gasping, shattered in the most exquisite way.

As the waves of ecstasy ebbed, leaving me spent and vulnerable, I let out a laugh. "Hotel sex," I managed between ragged breaths, "is still the best sex in the world."

Lior chuckled, his amusement warm against the damp skin of my thigh. "Only the best for you, baby," he said, untangling me from my binds with gentle efficiency, his eyes holding mine with the kind of love I was still getting used to receiving.

He scooped me into his arms and pulled the bed covers over us.

Our morning might have been steeped in hedonism, but it was the quiet moments I spent in his embrace that meant everything to me.

"We should get ready so we're not late," he said.

"Hmm…" That was all he was getting from me after destroying my ability for cognitive activity.

He pressed his fingers against my sides, tickling me.

"Damn you. Can a guy not enjoy a moment of peace in his husband's arms?"

Lior hooked his thumb under my chin to make me look up at him. "It was your third moment of peace that brought us here."

I shrugged. "What can I say? You make me horny."

Before Lior could say anything, there was an insistent knock on the door. We looked at each other.

"Are you expecting anyone?" he asked.

I shook my head, trying to hold onto the delicate thread of afterglow that still clung to me. "No," I replied.

With a sigh, I untangled myself from the bedding and Lior's embrace, slipping into my robe as he did the same. The fabric felt cool against my heated skin as I tied the sash around my waist, knotting it with finality.

"All right," I said, a soft resignation in my tone as I approached the door. "Let's see what catastrophe awaits." I drew back the bolt and there stood Lex, Emery, and a frazzled River.

They burst into the room, a whirlwind of worry and desperation.

"They're lost," River repeated, his voice a notch higher than usual, "the wedding bands."

I leaned against the doorframe, crossing my arms over my chest.

"What do you mean?" I asked.

"I can't find them. I looked everywhere." River paced the room back and forth. "Adam is going to be so upset. Oh god, what if he decides he doesn't want to marry me." He stopped and looked at Lior. "He wouldn't do that, would he?"

Lior shook his head. "I don't think anything—bar a natural catastrophe happening on the island—would stop him from marrying you today."

"Can we get married without rings?"

"You can, but you won't need to. The rings are not lost," I said, my tone light and sure. The room fell silent, three pairs of eyes fixed on me, searching for the joke or the lie in my words. But it was neither.

"Lior has them." I couldn't help but let my grin widen as I watched Lior's expression shift from serene to mock exasperation.

Adam had insisted on Lior being the keeper of the rings, citing everyone else's immaturity and track record for losing things.

"Of course," River murmured, relief washing over his features so quickly it was like watching a storm clear. "I don't know how I forgot that." He dropped onto a nearby chair like a deflated balloon. "I'm so sorry, guys. I didn't mean—"

"Hey," Lex said, crouching next to River. "It's your wedding day. You're allowed to feel a little out of sorts. That's why we're all here."

River looked at Lex and nodded.

"Okay, now that the mystery has been solved, why don't you all go back to your suites while my husband and I get dressed." I turned to River. "Don't worry, I'm not shirking my best man responsibilities. Give me thirty, and I'll meet you in your suite."

"Okay." He stood, a new spring on his step, as he practically glided toward the door.

The door had barely closed behind the retreating figures of Lex, Emery, and a visibly calmer River when I spun to face Lior and let my robe slide down my body onto the carpet.

Lior's gaze was like a heated caress and the unmissable tent in his robe gave me a new sense of urgency...or purpose, more like.

I caught him by the wrist and tugged him toward the

bathroom, our feet barely touching the plush carpet as we moved.

"You heard me. You have half an hour," I said.

"For what?"

"Shower. Now," I commanded, my voice low and husky, leaving no room for argument.

Lior's response was a throaty laugh, his desire evident as he allowed me to pull him into the steam-filled enclosure.

Without another word, I turned around to face the tiled wall and whispered the words I knew would finally make Lior lose all control. "Fuck me until I can't do anything but squirm every time I sit down for the next twelve hours."

And so, under the hot spray of water that washed over us, my husband complied, our bodies moving together at a pace set by him for him.

It was a minor miracle my body found the energy for another orgasm. It was a small one compared to the ones from last night that had made me shudder uncontrollably every time Lior massaged my prostate with his cock.

I didn't want to leave him after we'd gotten dressed. Not when he looked like suit porn. Even if my body was well beyond sated, I could stare at my husband looking that good and smelling even better for hours.

"Go on," he said. "Go be the best best man for River. I'll drop the rings in your pocket when you walk down the aisle."

I rested my hands on his waist and reached up to him on tiptoes, seeking his mouth for one last kiss.

"I love you so much, Lior."

"I love you too, Noah."

PART 3

ADAM

My hands trembled as I straightened my tie in front of the mirror, the knots of anxiety in my stomach tangling tighter with each passing second.

My reflection stared back at me, a man on the cusp of one of the biggest life changes a person could make, if you discounted the tiny detail of my late sexual awakening, of course.

The room hummed with the silent energy of anticipation, the tropical breeze from the open window doing little to cool my flushed skin.

I tried to focus on the simple task before me, but my mind was a whirlwind of memories, the ghost of an alternate reality where this wedding never came to be lingering in the periphery of my thoughts.

"Steady," I whispered, watching my lips form the word without sound. I closed my eyes for a brief moment, inhaling the salt-tinged air.

I could almost taste the sweet floral notes that wafted

from the arrangements outside, intermingled with the faintest hint of citrus from the trees dotting the resort grounds.

When I opened my eyes, there was a conviction that hadn't been there before. It wasn't just about standing here, about waiting to walk down the aisle toward River. It was about every step we'd taken together since we were kids, every late-night talk and shared laugh, every kiss, touch, or promise.

A soft knock on the door jolted me from my thoughts.

"Come in," I called, smoothing down the front of my shirt one last time.

The door opened, and though I expected to see my mother or perhaps Lex, ready to offer brotherly encouragement or step into his best man duties and re-straighten my tie, the sight of River standing there stole the breath from my lungs.

There was an unspoken rule, a superstition really, about not seeing each other before the ceremony, but in that instant, none of it mattered.

"River," I exhaled, hearing the relief in my voice.

"Hey," he replied, his own nerves apparent in the tightness around his eyes. "I just... I needed to see you, just for a second."

And with those words, any remaining doubts or uncertainties about the future collapsed. Because no matter what tradition said, it was this—our connection, our ability to turn to one another in moments of need—that was the essence of our relationship.

"I love you so much, Adam," he said, caressing my cheek.

"I love you too, River. Meet me at the altar?"

He stole a quick kiss and smiled. "You bet."

Moments later, laughter from River's adjoining suite,

muffled but unmistakable, drifted through the walls, wrapping around me like a comforting blanket.

The nerves that had settled in my stomach since I'd woken up calmed a fraction at the reminder that River was just as caught up in the whirlwind of emotions as I was.

A gentle tap on the door announced my next visitor.

"Adam?"

"Come in, Mom," I replied.

The door opened and in stepped my mother, her smile serene and radiant. She held out her arms, and I met her halfway into the kind of hug you could only ever receive from your mom.

"Look at you," she breathed, her eyes glistening with unshed tears. "My son, about to start a new chapter in his life. You look so handsome."

"Thanks, Mom." My throat tightened as I took her arm.

"Remember, love is like an anchor," she said as we began to walk out of the room, her voice steady and sure. "It holds fast against any storm. And I've never seen two people more anchored in each other than you and River."

I nodded, swallowing hard. I allowed myself to be led and comforted by her presence as we made our way down the hall toward the room where the ceremony would be held.

"Almost there," she whispered.

As we rounded the corner, the foyer opened into an expanse of expectant faces, all turned toward us. But it wasn't the sea of guests that caught my breath, it was Lex, standing off to the side, his role as best man worn like a badge of honor. His eyes met mine, and as it always was with us, there was no need for words. We'd been able to read each other's thoughts since before we could walk. There was no one else I would rather have standing by my side today.

The music started, so I held my mom's hand in mine, and we walked down the aisle, ready and excited to see my future husband again and make the promises we'd already made all those years ago when we were still kids.

We would always be each other's best friends no matter what.

Enjoying getting naked with him was a bonus.

When we reached the altar, Mom kissed my cheek before doing the same to Lex. She sat beside Dad and Grandma, pulling a small handkerchief from her purse and dabbing her eyes with it.

The music picked up again, and through the double doors, River made his entrance.

River's mom, a beacon of maternal elegance, took his arm, and together, they stepped into the sun-drenched aisle.

Time, traitorously, didn't stand still but seemed to pulse with the rhythm of my heartbeat.

My eyes followed their slow progression, each step a measured beat. This man who had patiently loved me from afar for so long and, when given the opportunity, loved me even more up close.

His hand rested delicately in his mother's, a silent testament to the nurturing love that had shaped him into the man he was today—the man I was about to call my husband.

He moved with a grace of a deep-seated certainty that whatever happened next, it was right—it was meant. And as he approached, my heart raced faster, but only because it always did when we were this close.

"River," I breathed his name like a prayer. A promise of forever love.

"Adam." His voice was a gentle wave washing over me.

"Hey. Told you I'd be here."

His smile was my undoing, and as a tear ran down my cheek, I looked into the depths of his eyes and found our future.

"Ready?" he asked, reaching for my cheek and pushing the stray tear away.

"Let's get married."

"Let's begin," the celebrant announced.

And as I took River's hand in mine, feeling the familiar yet exhilarating pulse of his heartbeat against my skin, I knew that every challenge we faced, every doubt we conquered, had led us here—to each other, this moment, this love that I had no doubt would endure beyond the final pages of any story we might write.

Thank you

It's been quite a journey for our three Spencer brothers, but especially for Adam and River. I loved writing their love story, and I hope you enjoyed reading it.